Acclaim for Van Allen's Ecstasy

"Using his narrator's memory gaps and obsessions, Tushinski creates his own syn-aesthetic symphonies and strange new melodies, a music of mania and loss. *Van Allen's Ecstasy* is a compelling contribution to the literature of madness and identity."

—Stephen Beachy
Author, *The Whistling Song* and *Distortion*

"*Van Allen's Ecstasy* explores the mutable boundaries between genius and insanity, and between obsession and delusion. This tale of a man who yearns to make his mark through music is by turns wry, spooky, and aching. It is a passionate novel about the passion of creativity."

—Jean Thompson
Author, *Who Do You Love* and *Wide Blue Yonder*

"This book is a fascinating entrée into the mind of Michael Van Allen, who has under-gone a nervous breakdown. Tushinski appropriately titles the three major sections of this evocative novel 'languor,' 'yearning,' and 'ecstasy' as he expertly interweaves the various, seemingly disparate, elements. He masterfully achieves a rich portrait of Mi-chael's internal struggle for sanity, as well as powerful characterizations of those around him. Tushinski's sensitive and confident command of language immediately engages the reader, transporting him or her to the denouement of this immensely satisfying novel."

—Jim Van Buskirk
Program Manager,
James C. Hormel Gay & Lesbian Center,
San Francisco Public Library

"'I remember and remember and remember,' Jim Tushinski writes, 'and the act of re-membering becomes a physical sensation, like drinking water to quench a thirst.' In *Van Allen's Ecstasy,* the act of reading, too, becomes a physical sensation. This is the story of Michael Van Allen, a man unable to create in a family of natural-born creators, a man yearning for the joy of unrestrained creative activity—ecstasy. What Michael doesn't know is that there is a price to pay for ecstasy.

We are lost with Michael in a story in a mist, feeling our way through place, time, and people that ought to be familiar, but aren't. This is a story about how we are who we are, even without all the memories and connections we depend upon every day to help us define ourselves. Tushinski has written in a prose that is by turns major-key bold and minor-key tentative in response to the estranged world we—the writer, the reader, and Michael Van Allen himself—must make familiar once again."

—Brian Bouldrey
Author, *Love, the Magician, Monster,* and *The Boom Economy*

"In *Van Allen's Ecstasy*, one hears a scream that is an expression at once of folly, rage, and a terrible ecstasy, all of which are born out of a revulsion for the way things are, the world's unaccountable refusal to satisfy the soul's need for purity and transcendence. That scream reverberates throughout the book. Instead of indulging in its emotion, however, *Van Allen's Ecstasy* risks austerity and an expressive restraint too challenging and complex to be mistaken for plainness. Its lyric moments, when they appear, are consequently all the more darkly luminous, in particular during the novel's final passages. In no sense a case or diagnostic study of a soul in extremity, Tushinski's novel evokes instead one young man's discovery of and longing for the mystic chord into which he would transform his life. But it also profoundly understands how much is forsaken when that chord at last begins to sound."

—Peter Weltner
Author, *The Risk of His Music* and *How the Body Prays*

495

Van Allen's Ecstasy

HARRINGTON PARK PRESS
Southern Tier Editions
Gay Men's Fiction
Jay Quinn, Executive Editor

Van Allen's Ecstasy

Jim Tushinski

Southern Tier Editions
Harrington Park Press®
An Imprint of The Haworth Press, Inc.
New York • London • Oxford

Published by

Southern Tier Editions, Harrington Park Press®, an imprint of The Haworth Press, Inc., 10 Alice Street, Binghamton, NY 13904-1580.

PUBLISHER'S NOTE
This is a work of fiction. Names, characters, places, and incidents either are the products of the author's imagination or are used fictitiously, and any resemblance to actual persons, living or dead, business establishments, events, or locales is entirely coincidental.

Portions of this book have appeared in somewhat different form in *His 3: Brilliant New Fiction by Gay Writers* (Faber & Faber).

Cover design by Cory Bernat.
Photographer: Steve Savage

Library of Congress Cataloging-in-Publication Data

Tushinski, Jim.
   Van Allen's ecstasy / Jim Tushinski.
     p. cm.
   ISBN 1-56023-455-5 (alk. paper)
   I. Title.
   PS3620.U84V36 2004
813'.6—dc21

                                 2003005271

For Ray Chance
XOXO

part one

languor

Mother is painting stars. She thinks I'm asleep on the couch, wrapped in a heavy blanket, but I watch her as she paints, peeking out from a half-open eye, seeing her through a blur of lashes. She stands quite still for minutes, stands in front of a large canvas painted a dark blue that's almost black. Then she moves to a particular spot and stabs her brush. I fall asleep. When I wake up, galaxies have appeared.

Yesterday, I was in the hospital.

I was in a room, standing in the middle where they left me, looking at the blank walls, the metal frame bed, a desk, a pen, a piece of paper. *Dear Paul.*

Was this my room? I couldn't pull my thoughts together. This place looked lived in, the sheets on the bed in disarray. I sat at the desk, not aware of how I got there, unable to recall walking across the room, pulling out the chair. The piece of paper was too white, the ink too blue.

Dear Paul. Underneath the words I wrote: *Who are you?*

I wrote it carefully, imitating the handwriting on the line above.

I'm in this room. Your name is written here. If this is my room, then I wrote your name. I know who you are.

I looked up. The window was high in the opposite wall, the glass embedded with wire. I tried, for a moment, to imagine what was outside, but all I could picture was an uneven, treeless place and a flat sky.

Before I was in this room, before I sat at this desk and wrote those words on that piece of paper, I was walking down a corridor. I heard noises, people talking, things moving around, but the noises didn't come all at once. They came in bits, weaving in and out of importance, balancing, then contrasting one another. I wanted to cry.

Next to me, a large man in white held my arm. I shuffled and the man was there to help me. That made sense. I leaned against the man, who was warm and hairy.

Before I was walking down the corridor, I remember being some-place else. Another room, bigger than the room with the desk. I was propped up on a bed, a hard bed with white, white sheets and railings on the side. A man leaned over me, shaving my face with an electric razor. Was this the same man who helped me down the corridor? I can't be sure. The man shaved me with the razor and I thought, *How come he's shaving me? Why can't I move my arms and legs?* He took a tissue and wiped away the saliva that ran from my open mouth.

All around me in this room I sensed other people in other beds just like mine. I couldn't see them because I couldn't turn my head, but I heard them thrashing around, moaning, or pulling on straps. I re-membered the sound of leather stretching.

I looked at myself in my mirror. My mirror. My room.

I was wearing a bright white gown tied at the back. My hair was black and thick but cropped close. My eyes stared back at me. Every so often I forced myself to close my mouth. I soon forgot, though, as I stared at my face. My mouth fell open again.

I mustn't be very old. That's not why I'm here. This isn't a nursing home. I'm younger than the man who brought me down the corridor. I'm a young man, really.

Looking at the room reflected in my mirror made me dizzy. I stepped back and lost my balance.

There were so many people in that place. They walked along the corridors or sat and chattered. Doctors and nurses walked past me, sometimes smiling and asking how I'm doing. Mostly, though, they seemed preoccupied.

The orderlies never asked me anything. They told me. *Sit down. Stop bothering him. Don't talk so loud.* When they weren't around, I hugged whoever was near me. I'm not sure why.

In the dayroom, a tall man watched television for hours at a time. I, on the other hand, watched the handsome disheveled man play a board game with the longhaired and gray old man. The old man was sweating, droplets falling onto the game board when he leaned in to move his marker. He wiped the drops away with a practiced motion of his arm.

The sunlight in the room grew yellow, imperceptible to everyone but me. When the sunlight was at its most yellow, when the shadows from the thin wire mesh in the windows grew longer across the floor, the other people in the dayroom became wrapped in a blurry halo that obscured their faces. When they moved past me, I almost didn't see them. They could be wind. I could be alone on a beach. Instead of waves, I heard chords of music.

In the light. There was a man. He seemed to live in the light, this man. I wasn't sure if he was real, but that didn't stop me from participating.

His name is Sasha and he's not very tall. The striking oval of his face tapered into a trim brown Vandyke and a long mustache waxed to a point at each end. He held himself a bit haughtily, or maybe it was just confidence, yet there was something childlike about him, a strange sort of tenderness. I could see his long-fingered hands. He smiled and spoke in high-pitched and nervous French. *His accent is Slavic,* I thought, then was frightened by my matter of factness.

"What could be worse than Moscow in the summer?" Sasha asked. He wore old-fashioned, expensive clothes tailored to fit his small frame—a frock coat and vest and a shirt with a starched collar. "What could be worse?"

In the reception area, I floated a few inches above the floor. It really wasn't a pleasant feeling. I had so little control—pushed around and tethered like a balloon. The pills kicked in while I sat waiting in my room and now the air looked hazy. People had halos of light around them, like headaches made visible. The halos throbbed if I looked at them too long. If I looked at the people. At the halos, too. Through the foggy air, I saw a tired, uncomfortable-looking woman in a heavy wool coat. Her halo was gray. She wore glasses with big, light blue frames that helped round her thin face. She smiled.

I knew it was Mother. People and things came back to me in no particular order and just as quickly left me, but she didn't need to remind me who she was.

"The doctor says there's no reason to keep you here anymore," Mother told me. We sat in the car. It was cold.

I didn't remember walking out of the hospital or across the parking lot. I didn't remember opening the car door. I could see the hospital from where I sat. I could breathe on the window and watch my breath condense. A gray layer of hardened snow covered the ground. The other windows started fogging up.

"He says with the medication and therapy you'll be fine. He has faith in you. He says you're a survivor." She pushed a button and a noise filled the car, followed by a jet of warm air. The windows melted before me and I could see the hospital again, a dark old building made of sweating stones. I thought about laughing, thought about reaching out to see if the windows might still be there. Then I thought about the act of laughing and the idea of the window. The air got warmer in the car.

She looked at me.

"We did this for your own good," she said, her voice trembling a little. "You needed help."

I wasn't sure how to respond, so I said nothing. She pushed another button, stepped on a pedal. The car moved.

"You don't look well, Michael. Did they feed you at all? You look so thin."

"Just tired," I said.

Mother stopped glowing as we drove away from the hospital. I looked at her—recognized the tilt of her head, her gray and black hair, her knuckles straining from her grip on the car's steering wheel. These things seemed natural, familiar. Perhaps it was the pills, pushing me into a safe place. When I smiled, my mouth never seemed to stop moving.

"Your father couldn't come," Mother said, not looking at me, intent on the road ahead. I tried to watch the road as well, but I began rushing away as the road moved toward me, one movement canceling

the other and leaving the car suspended. Only when I looked at
Mother did we seem to move.

"It's difficult for him to come home when he's touring," she said.

I can't picture my father or the places where Mother and I are
headed, but nevertheless I'm soothed by the certainty that everything
will be clear in time. The interior of the car, the cold gray upholstery,
the blue tinting along the top of the windows, the black laces weaving
in and out of the steering wheel wrap—all these seemed as familiar to
me as my hospital room.

"Yes," I said, "I understand."

She smiled, glanced away from the road for an instant and looked
at me. I understand. Yes. I understand what words to say so Mother
will smile. She loosened her grip on the steering wheel. Her shoulders
relaxed. Radiating out from the corner of her eyes, a web of wrinkles
remained when her smile faded.

"You remember what it's like when he's touring," she said, and I
understood something in her voice, hopeful and trembling, transmit-
ted to me at a frequency I couldn't quite hear. *You remember,* she said
again, but her mouth hadn't moved. The heated air blew from the
vent, hitting my face. I wanted to blink, but couldn't.

"Yes," I said. "Touring . . ."

I let out a sigh. Mother nodded, then shook her head while she
smiled again.

This seemed so easy, like a game. Mother spoke and I replied.
There was no need to say anything new. I reused her words and she
smiled, and despite my numbness I knew that to make her smile I had
to choose my repetition carefully. I must choose and react—sigh, gesture, frown—and then listen.

I was confident now. Confident and numb.

I looked out the window.

The car wasn't moving, though the wet streets and traffic lights
flew past with a measured regularity. I was caught between the push
and the pull. Between the roadside and the car, as immobile as we
were, Sasha was standing.

What could be worse than Moscow in the summer? Sasha asked, and I
heard my own voice speaking some of the words along with him.

"What could be worse?" I said.

Flocks of pigeons blocking out the sky, fouling the Kremlin and the palaces with their droppings—and the constant buzzing of flies, those horrible, swarming Moscow flies. What could be worse?

"Nothing," Mother said, delighted. "Touring is the worst."

I turned to look at her, knowing that the turning of my head would make Sasha go away and make the car move again.

The layout of Mother's house was unfamiliar. There seemed to be endless rooms opening off other rooms full of doors, stairs, and carefully arranged furniture. The walls were off-white, the colors coming from bold splashes of blue and red and yellow in the furniture's fabrics. I followed Mother as she walked and then turned toward me, to see if anything like recognition would appear on my face. I kept my face smooth. She spoke the names of the rooms as we entered them and made a spreading gesture with her arms, presenting the rooms to me.

"Living room," she said. "Family room, dining room, kitchen."

We climbed some stairs and I saw a hallway, more doors, and behind the doors—more rooms, more off-white walls, more gestures, more words. The carpet in the hallway was a different shade of plush off-white. I stared at it, focused on the twists of carpet fiber and the way light reflected. Mother bravely moved forward into another room.

"This is your room," she said.

Mother is painting stars.

"Mother," I say, and she stiffens, slowly setting her brush on the small table. She doesn't turn around.

"This one's quite large," she says, her tone clipped and a bit distracted, as if she's speaking to herself. "They've become larger over the last year."

For a moment, we're both silent. She stares at the blue-black night full of stars. I watch the back of her head.

"What do you do with them when they're finished?" I ask.

"Each one is different, you know." She turns around to face me, her eyes locking on mine. I can't look away.

"If I like them," she says, "if they're really good, I give them to my agent, who sells them. But mostly, I paint over them." She turns back to the canvas. "Until I get it right." She picks up her brush, dips it in deep blue paint, then touches a spot on the canvas.

It seems like a message, some kind of cue. I go upstairs.

"Michael," she calls, and it sounds like a warning.

"I'm thirsty," I tell her.

It's my fault, really. She doesn't trust me, can't let me out of her sight. If I'm upstairs too long, she'll call for me again, then come up to see what I'm doing. It's my own fault. I should have known that lying and pretending to understand takes its toll.

I don't know how long I've been upstairs or when Mother came into the room. From where I'm sitting, at the kitchen table, I can see her holding a telephone receiver toward me, her hand covering the mouthpiece. "You have a phone call," she says. Her voice is flat and too polite. I don't remember hearing the telephone ring.

I hesitate. I'm sure I've talked on the telephone before, though I don't recall when. I understand the principle, but the technique is elusive.

"It's Paul," she says.

I look directly at Mother, see her mouth move but hear no sound. I read her lips, hesitate an instant more, then stand up and take the receiver.

"Yes," I say, but choke a bit and repeat, "yes," afraid I haven't been heard.

"Mike," the voice from the receiver says, racing up the syllable of my name. "How are you?" I imagine him from his voice, see him as dark and compact with a single, thick eyebrow and a full, reassuring mouth. The voice tries to sound casual, but I suppose the call is difficult for the voice—for Paul. I see him in a faraway place, a place with no walls, no furniture, no sky. The air in that place glows.

"I'm sort of tired," I say slowly.

"When are you coming home, Mike?" Paul's voice asks.

The word *home* makes a sound in my ear and I move the receiver away. Mother sees this and frowns. I want her to go. Although I'm not sure who I'm talking to, I know this is private. I frown back at Mother and wave my hand at her as though she were a troublesome fly.

"I'm home now," I tell Paul without really thinking about it.

Paul says nothing for a while, then speaks my name very softly. "I miss you so much," he says.

His words make my heart pound and I'm not sure what I feel. I can't miss someone I barely remember, but I say what seems right, what Paul hopes for, and what I suspect is true.

"I miss you, too."

I smile. The words are mine even if they don't make much sense. Mother won't stop looking at me. She seems quite pale.

"I was hoping to speak to your mother," Paul says. "Is she there?"

"Yes," I say and hold the receiver toward her. "He wants to talk to you, too."

She hesitates. I can see her hand crumple a dishrag, then she moves a few steps forward and takes the receiver from me.

"Yes," she says, but looks at me. I walk away, across the dining room, into the living room where I sit on the sofa. Despite Mother's attempt to speak quietly, most of her words reach me.

"That's not really a possibility," she says. Then, after a pause, "Don't be ridiculous."

Paul seems to be doing most of the talking. Mother is quiet for a while, then she says abruptly, "I certainly can't stop you, but perhaps you should consider other people's feelings."

I can't make out what else she says for a while. Then I hear, "Yes, well, that's what *you* say." She sounds bored and her tone is somewhat final, then she laughs and a chill shoots right through me.

When she comes back into the living room, nothing about her seems different, but the chill stays.

"Didn't he want to talk to me some more?" I ask.

She smiles a tight little smile and shakes her head. "No," she says.

"What did he want?"

The telephone rings again, sounding too loud. Mother hurries back into the kitchen.

"Yes," she says, then lowers her voice.

When she returns, she says, "Wrong number. Let's go for a drive, shall we? You can help me buy groceries. Getting out will do you good."

"What did Paul want to talk to you about?"

"I'm not even sure," she says. "He's a little odd."

"He asked me when I was coming home."

For a moment, she is absolutely still.

"That *is* odd," she says at last. "After all, he called you here." She stands there looking at me, then asks, "How well do you remember him?"

The chill runs through my shoulders, making them twitch. The hairs on the back of my neck tingle.

"Are you cold?" she asks and I shake my head, managing a smile and a shrug.

"I remember him . . . very well," I say. I try to picture him but all I can conjure is a general impression—stocky with black curly hair. His face, though, is still blank. Everything's there—eyes, nose, mouth—but nothing's distinctive. "When I hear his voice," I say, "things come back to me."

"That's good." She seems to speak with conviction. "I'm curious," she says. "Do you remember more about Paul than you remember about this house, say, or your father or me?"

I can't think fast enough, and both Mother and I know my pause goes on too long.

"About the same," I say. "Things are getting a lot clearer."

"Your father will be so happy to see how well you're recovering. I think it hit him hardest. Not that we weren't all concerned, Michael, I certainly didn't mean that, but your father . . ." She stops and seems lost for a moment. "Well," she says, "shall we go for a drive?"

Mother bustles herself and me into coats, grabs her purse and keys, and as we're heading out the door, the telephone rings again. I look at Mother, making a movement to go back and answer it, but she closes the door behind her and locks it.

"I'm not expecting any important calls. Are you?" she says. "The message center will get it."

As we pull out of the driveway, I can hear the telephone as it rings and rings and rings in the empty house.

"Michael," a woman's voice says. "Michael, wake up." Someone is shaking me, but I can't open my eyes very far and my head seems tender and enlarged. A woman with gray and black hair is standing next to the bed, her hand resting on my shoulder. "Karl and Amy are here. Sara, too. It's dinnertime."

"What?" I try to say. "Sleeping." I can't keep my eyes open, so I close them and hope she will leave. Just as I drift away into the darkness, someone shakes me again, this time almost violently. I open my eyes and the woman is still there, not a part of some dream, as I had hoped. She looks at me, annoyed, perhaps, or just concerned.

"You've been sleeping for hours," she says. "Everyone is here to see you."

"Go away," I tell her, but she won't.

My brother and sister are here for dinner. At least that's who Mother says they are. I suppose the woman with my brother has to be his girlfriend. Or wife. Mother didn't say. We're all sitting in the living room and my sister Sara looks at me strangely, as if I've done something wrong or am emitting an unpleasant odor. She's older than me and her hair is unruly, falling away from her head in thick curls which she pushes this way and that. My brother Karl is taller than I am, maybe younger, but maybe not, with black, shiny hair and blue eyes I can't stop looking at. When he talks to me, his eyes won't look away and won't let mine look away either.

"You look wonderful," the other woman says. "So rested."

By process of elimination, she is Amy. She's blonde and touches my brother too often.

Before we all sit down for dinner, I excuse myself.

"I have to wash my hands," I say.

"Karl, go with him," Mother says, but my sister laughs. It's a cruel laugh.

"Really," she says. "He's not an invalid, Mother."

"I have to wash my hands," I say and slip upstairs to navigate the off-white hallways until I find the room I woke up in. I close the door, sit on the bed. *Remember,* I think, *remember, remember, remember. Something. Anything.* The panic slowly rises inside me, demanding that I scream. On the desk are a plastic orange bottle and an overnight bag. I walk over to the desk. The label on the bottle says MICHAEL VAN ALLEN and I know this is me, so I spill a little white tablet onto my palm.

"Michael," Mother calls from downstairs, "are you coming?"

The pill goes down with difficulty, leaving me coughing and flushed. I sit on the bed again, close my eyes. My breathing grows steady. The edge of my pain softens and fades away. Is it the pills working so quickly or just my anticipation of them?

Someone knocks on the door. "It's Karl," he says. "Are you OK?"

"Yes." I return the plastic container to the overnight bag and hurry to open the door. He's standing there, leaning against the wall, his hands in his pockets, with a casualness I can't help admiring since it's something I'm sure I lack. His face—it looks like my face in a way, but there's such a great difference, too. It's as if my face was modified, perfected. Memories and past experiences are beneath the features, not exactly visible, but sparkling out of those eyes. His hair is so black but the light, even the weak, unspecified light of the hallway, touches it with highlights of almost blue. His eyes speak to me. I should be able to translate but can't. I want to touch his hair, his cheek, but can't.

"Mom's worried, you know how she is," he says.

"Yes." It seems the easiest response.

"Hell, we're all worried," he says and then moves toward me. I take a step back. Karl stops and I see concern in his eyes, see a frown cross his lips. He holds out his hand.

"Mikey," he says, as though approaching a frightened pet, "come on." He smiles and the smile is so sad. "Let's go downstairs."

I reach up to take his hand and when we touch, my fingers tingle. Suddenly he seems quite familiar to me.

Throughout the meal I hear the conversation from a great distance, realizing I'm being addressed directly only when the pauses between the sentences become too long. No one else seems to notice the amount of time between a question and my answer. Maybe for them it's as if no time passes at all. When Mother goes into the kitchen, my brother leans over and pours me some wine. I notice a bluish tinge to his jaw where he shaved. I want to touch it, feel how smooth it is.

"Drink up," he says.

"Is that a good idea?" Amy asks. "Isn't he on medication?"

"A little wine won't hurt him."

He leans closer, speaks low in my ear. "Thickens the blood," he says.

His voice sends a warm shock through me. My brother is so close to me, close enough to touch. Should I kiss him? Instead, I reach for the wine and take a sip. I lower the glass, everything happening in slow motion, and again I watch my panic grow, as if I'm detached from it. The liquid slides down my throat, burning.

Mother comes into the room with a large box and sets it in front of me on the table. Inside are a number of smaller boxes, beautifully wrapped. The box is big. I know this, but now it seems so small and far away. The air begins to fill with the strange light. It envelops my family with a familiar and faint glow. I smile, a little frightened, and drain my wine glass.

"Merry Christmas," Amy says. "A little late."

"You shouldn't be drinking, Michael," Mother says. "Not with your medication." Then to my brother: "Don't give him any more."

"Open ours first," Karl says.

My sister stares at me from across the table.

I reach for the box Amy holds out, but it doesn't seem to have any solidity to it. My fingers pass right through and I watch it drop onto the table, upsetting the salt and pepper shakers.

"Goodness!" Amy exclaims. She picks up the package and looks confused, watching me.

"I don't think he even knows he dropped it," Sara says in disgust.

Pushing through the heavy glow, I reach out again and take the present, slowly, deliberately. I try to untie the ribbon and peel off the paper but my fingers won't move in the right way. They feel thick—bloated and soft. A string of saliva hangs in the air and drops onto the

package. It takes me a long time to understand where it came from. I try to move my jaw, to stop the string of drool. With an effort, I succeed.

"Jesus," Sara says.

Now I start to cry. My words come out in an angry slur, but neither I nor any of my family can understand what I'm trying to say. Amy looks down at her plate, then takes the present and unwraps it. When she finishes, she sets it in front of me. Inside is a small music box. She lifts the lid and a tune begins to play. A tinny, unrecognizable melody.

"It's your favorite song," Karl says halfheartedly.

I stand up, knocking my chair backward and surprising myself. I'm not sure where the energy comes from or why this anger makes it up through the glowing light. A scream sits inside me, waiting.

Mother looks terrified and beaten. She clutches the tablecloth, covers her mouth.

"Michael, please," she says.

"Just calm down," Karl says, touching me. "Take it easy." Then he turns to Mother and asks, "Does he need his medication?"

I stumble and fall forward.

A blanket covers me, pulled up around my neck. I lie in a bedroom. It's dark. The clock says 2:15. My head is clear, as if a large space exists there, an open window with a breeze blowing the curtains inward. A blue sky. No clouds.

I sit up.

I don't hear any movement, no sounds except the ticking of many clocks and a distant hum.

I get out of bed. The fear fills me up. Like a drop of oil on a clean white cloth, it saturates me.

Where am I? What's my name?

I walk to the hallway, grabbing onto the door frame to steady myself. Nothing looks familiar.

As I move down the hall, I notice a bathroom to my left. I go in. Close the door. Sit on the toilet in the dark. And I breathe—rapidly at first, then forcing myself to go slower and slower. Taking air in, filling my lungs, pushing the panic out. Slowly, slowly. As suddenly as the fear comes on, it subsides, leaving behind the house, the bathroom, my name. This is my home, yet it is not my home. The people at dinner are my family, yet they are not my family. *Dear Paul,* I think, *who are you? Where are you?*

Inside the medicine cabinet is an orange plastic pill bottle. I remove the top and spill one white tablet into my palm, then pop the pill into my mouth. For a moment, I think about swallowing it, knowing the comforting numbness that will come, but at the same time I try to picture Paul and can imagine only a shadowy shape, can barely hear his voice. I cough the pill into the sink where it slips down the drain, enveloped in a glob of saliva. Paul is slipping away, too. I hang onto the sides of the sink as if that will keep him here.

I don't want to sleep.

2

The waiting room swims in shades of brown. It resembles some-one's parlor—comfortable chairs, a couch, and a fireplace mantle.

As Mother and I climbed the wide steep steps to the doctor's office, I noticed graceful curling details along the roofline, a heavy, ornate door, multipaned windows, like a gingerbread house from some fairy tale I can't remember. Mother had punched a series of buttons on a keypad. A buzzer sounded and she pushed the door open. Inside, a hallway stretched to a closed door at the back of the house. Mother steered me to the right, into the beige and taupe and burnt umber, where we now sit in our warm coats, Mother flipping through a mag-azine and me fingering the elaborate pattern woven into the arm of the big brown chair. Now and then, Mother looks up from her flip-ping, looks at me and gestures to her mouth. I close mine. The clock ticks and Mother nods.

I look at some magazines piled on an end table near me and linger on the bright covers showing people whose hair is perfect and whose clothes fit so well. I may have looked this way once.

I stand up, take off my coat, placing it on the chair, walk over to a mirror above the mantle. I hear Mother stop flipping and sense her looking at me—something I'll have to get used to. In the mirror, I see my eyes. They're not blue like my brother's, but a muddy brown, like the color of the waiting room walls. My hair grows out unevenly. I re-member shaving this morning, but I see dark stubble. If I ever looked like the people on the magazines, it was a long time ago. My face shows no poise, my posture no ease. I have to close my mouth again. Mother still watches me. Her magazine is silent.

I'm just looking in the mirror, I think, imagining this thought has a physical presence and that I can propel it with the power of my will into Mother's ear. She'll hear it, a little voice, barely audible. The flipping starts again and I smile into the mirror.

"Hello, Doctor," Mother says, and the flipping stops. I turn and see a handsome man with gray hair and beard standing in the doorway to the hall. He smiles and extends his hand to me. I notice his wrist is thick and hairy. He's looking at me but speaks to Mother.

"Mrs. Van Allen," he says, "how are you? Hello, Mike."

His hand is still extended, so I move toward him and grasp it, though I can't apply much pressure. It's the pills, I suspect. Mother has control of them now.

"Do you remember me at all?" he asks, still smiling.

I smile back and notice that his hair is perfect, like the magazine covers.

"A little," I say, a small lie. The doctor's eyes are blue, but not like the blue of my brother's eyes, and I can tell he knows I'm lying.

"I'm Dr. Jamison," he says and releases my hand. "Shall we go back to my office?" Dr. Jamison gestures down the hall. He hasn't stopped smiling. I wonder if he can or ever will.

Stop smiling, I think and send the thought to him with a slight crinkling of my brow. He gestures again, the smile not faltering. Perhaps I need more practice with men. I follow Dr. Jamison down the hall to the closed door at the end.

His office is not brown.

The first thing I notice is the light, coming in from the double glass doors that lead to a little garden. The furniture is black and soft, but it picks up the light, seems to shine, looking slippery. The walls glow. The doors to the garden are ajar and occasionally a fly shoots into the room, bouncing off the glass with a fat buzz as it tries to find its way back outside.

"Sit down," Dr. Jamison says, indicating the leather couch. "Is it too bright in here for you?"

I start to answer him but can't decide what to say. The light is blinding but beautiful as well.

"You're squinting," he says and strides over to the glass doors, pulls a drape across them, and disappears into the darkness. A desk lamp clicks on and I see that the doctor is now standing across the room with his hand still on the lamp's switch.

"Sit down," he says.

There are no pictures on his walls. I sit on the couch and face him as he takes his place in a chair. Behind him is an abstract wall hanging made from orange and brown yarn. The yarn twists, but the pattern is uninteresting, so I look at the doctor's perfect beard and wonder if it's soft or coarse.

"It's been quite a while since we've talked," he says. "You've been in the hospital three months." He looks at me and remains quiet for a long time. There seems to be no way to respond to him, so I wait out the pause.

"How much do you remember?"

"Flashes," I say. "Little pictures. Bits of things."

"Such as?"

I have to think about this for a while because no image comes to mind.

"Things don't surprise me much."

"What things?" His voice is smooth and his words flow quite naturally from my own. It doesn't sound like a question. It feels like I'm talking with myself.

"The way Mother looks." I pause again until an image comes to me. "The colors in her paintings. My brother's lips."

"His lips?"

"His eyes," I say, and it's true. "I meant his eyes."

The doctor doesn't say anything, just looks at me.

"They're so blue," I say.

"And the color in your mother's painting?"

"The blue," I say and then can't think of anything else.

"Are you having trouble concentrating?" the doctor asks. "How do you feel?"

"A little tired."

"Do you have any questions for me?" he says. "Anything you want to know?"

I don't understand why it's difficult to say this, but the word comes out so soft and broken that I have to clear my throat and repeat it a little louder. "Why," I say, "why I went to the hospital. Mostly just that."

"You had a breakdown. At one of your father's recitals. You don't remember any of it?"

"Just when they took me to the hospital."

"They? Who?"

"I'm not sure. More than two of them, I think."

"You started screaming. Some ushers had to remove you."

I can't picture this. The image is so absurd that I almost laugh but catch myself. "Was the concert stopped?" I try not to smile.

"No. Do you think it should have been?"

"What? I don't think so."

"It shouldn't have been stopped?" the doctor asks, and I'm not sure what he means by this. *No* seems the safest word, so I say it.

Dr. Jamison just looks at me for a very long time. He gives the impression he's content to wait until our time is up, but of course, he's not. His smile broadens.

"Am I going to have to do all the talking?" he finally asks. "I can just sit here and look at you if that's what you'd prefer."

"Why was I screaming?" It comes out of me fast, as though I were expelling the thought.

"I don't know, Mike. Do you remember anything at all?"

"No," I say, "I really don't, Doctor. I'm sorry."

"Nothing to apologize about, Mike. You do remember the drive to the hospital, though. All right. What do you remember about it? Do you remember the kind of car you rode in?"

Sirens. I remember sirens. An ambulance? I also remember, as clearly as I can remember anything, sitting in the backseat. Do ambulances have backseats? I remember wind. A convertible?

"Just a car," I say. "A car."

"Can you think of any reason why you would start screaming like that?"

I try. I really do try. Was I in pain? Was it something my father did? Nothing comes. No image, no impression, no snatch of remembered conversation. At Mother's house . . . at home . . . Mother showed me a photograph of my father, one on a compact disc cover that read *Douglas Van Allen,* and I try to picture him sitting at a piano on a concert hall stage, try to picture him moving, speaking, try to see him as anything else except that photograph. I shake my head. There's nothing but that frozen, powerful suggestion of a smile, his eyes downcast just enough so you can't see their color, his thick straight hair brushed back, the careful gray at his temples looking as though it was applied by a makeup artist, along with a touch of lip color.

"Mike," Dr. Jamison says, "have you ever heard of Alexander Scriabin? Does that name mean anything to you?"

"I think so," I say, and it's the truth again. I've heard the name before. "Should it?"

"He was a Russian composer. Your father was playing one of Scriabin's piano sonatas when you had your breakdown."

"Was he there?" I ask.

"Scriabin? No, Mike, he's been dead since 1915 or so."

There's little else to say. It's hard to follow our conversation because my attention incessantly wanders over the objects and textures in the room—the twisting orange yarn on the wall, the tweed of the doctor's jacket, an unopened envelope far away on his desk. I try to keep my eye movement to a minimum so Dr. Jamison won't notice, always returning to his face when I stray, afraid he'll ask me what I'm looking at and afraid I won't remember the object's name or how to describe the texture in words. There are two worlds now—one exterior to me where everything is hard and bright and labeled, where I'm expected to know things and to keep long lists of names, and the other world that looks out onto this exterior world yet doesn't exist in the same way. This other world is sometimes empty and sometimes teeming with sensations, but it's a place where names are admitted reluctantly. Maybe this is why talking tires me. I have to force the names inside, then attach them to sensations, infecting them and turning them into hard, dead husks. Like a sneeze, I eject something dead into the outer world where it becomes a sound, representing the sensation but not resembling it at all.

"Mike," Dr. Jamison says.

"I'm sorry." I bring my attention back to him, to the gray hair and his lips, so full and moist and red, set in his perfect beard. He's not smiling now.

"Do you understand what happened to you?" he asks. "Why you can't remember everything?"

"The treatment," I say. "I went to the hospital for this treatment." Dr. Jamison nods. "Because I started screaming. It rearranged things in my head."

"A temporary side effect. In time everything will come back to you. For a while, though, we're going to work on retrieving some of those memories, try to coax them out. It's confusing now. I understand that. But compared to the state you were in before the treatments, you've really improved. You're calm, reasonably coherent. How are you sleeping?"

I try to recall last night and realize I can only remember waking up disoriented. Logic dictates that I got into bed and lay there waiting for sleep. If I had any difficulties, any tossing about for a comfortable position, any bleary and maddening hours of staring at the ceiling, I should remember. The ceiling over my bed, was it prickly or smooth? Is there a lighting fixture there? What color are the walls?

"Fine," I say. "Like a baby."

"Good. Before you were hospitalized, you suffered from severe insomnia."

Sleep seems so natural and yet even as I think this, I know the symptoms of not sleeping just as well. Is insomnia as natural to me as sleep? Is there pleasure involved in the waiting, in the dull pounding of exhaustion that comes with the daylight? I imagine the moment when adrenaline surges like a cymbal crash and you believe you can go on without sleep forever. The world seems sharper, focused, as though you turned a magnifying glass on the air and saw everything—molecules, bacteria, dust motes—whirling around you. I remember this. It isn't some delusion I've conjured from a zapped and fried mind. I remember it.

"Sometimes," I say, "I didn't sleep for days."

Dr. Jamison smiles again. I watch his lips and my face flushes.

"It's coming back to you, isn't it?"

"Parts."

"Let's try something," Dr. Jamison says. "Close your eyes. Lean back."

I do as he tells me. His voice sounds so close in the dark, as if he were next to me or inside me.

"Relax," the voice says. "Breathe deeply . . . in . . . and out. Breathe in . . . and out . . ."

I hear the voice repeating the instructions, but soon it moves away, sounding as though it and I are in an enormous cavern. I hear the voice retreating, but the acoustics of this place keep the voice clear. Gradually the blackness turns gray, brightening, but revealing nothing. The voice keeps repeating its phrases and I keep breathing to the voice, seeing nothing, but feeling the air and hearing it rush into my lungs, then out of them.

Another voice, closer to me, begins speaking, gaining volume with each high-pitched, impassioned word.

"Life," the other voice says, "full of miracles, revelations ever newer and deeper and deeper, limitless and inexhaustible."

One area of the gray lightens faster than the rest and gradually Sasha fades into view, floating in the void, dressed in black evening attire. Light pours from his eyes. The effect would be demonic, but the light is not fierce and Sasha is too slight, too delicate to appear evil. His skin is made of exquisitely thin and translucent glass. His auburn hair is brushed back from his high forehead and falls into a casual part with uneven waves on either side. His Vandyke, his waxed mustache, the elegant arches of his eyebrows all reflect the skin's glow, their colors warmed by it. He wears a crisp white collar and a green and red and gold plaid cravat that seems made of stained glass.

"I call you to life, *ô forces mystérieuses*," Sasha intones, stretching his arms before him. "Rise up from the secret depths of the creative spirit."

"Obviously the product of a feverish period of creativity," Dad says. I can sense him standing behind me, but I can't turn around. I'm afraid there's no one there. "He believed the music was a divine gift. Luckily, the piece is so good you can ignore the poem as the scribblings of a deluded egomaniac."

God, how I wish I could turn around.

"Michael," Dr. Jamison says. "You must be tired."

I'm sitting on the couch again. The great space, the voices, Sasha, and Dad are gone.

"You've done really well," he says, standing up and offering me his hand. "It'll become easier, don't worry. Are you feeling all right?"

"Yes," I say. "Just tired."

"Then I'll see you in two days." He gestures to the door.

As we walk down the hall to the front room and to Mother waiting in the brown, I'm too tired to panic. If I scream now, it will burn in my throat like bile.

"So what do you want to do?" Mother asks me. She asks every day, mostly after we've been sitting for a while. Mother reads the paper, tidies up the coffee table, does whatever she can think of to keep herself busy while I sit and stare. It worries her, I know. She doesn't like to be idle. I, on the other hand, find the quiet and stillness calming. I don't mind doing nothing at all. I can think and sometimes, in those long stretches of silence, I can remember things.

Dr. Jamison's room seems more inviting this time—the light less intense. He leaves the draperies open and the smells and sounds of the garden conspire to pull my attention from him. I have to remind myself to look him in the eyes, appear to focus.

"How are you getting on with your family?" he asks when we have settled into our places.

"Good," I say. "Fine."

"Any episodes—panic attacks? Are you depressed?"

"No," I say. "Well, sometimes I forget everything again, but it all comes back. I just have to wait."

"Good." He nods. "That's normal. When the memories come back, do you remember more than before?"

I have to think about that—have to try to remember whether or not I remembered. This strikes me as absurd so I start to laugh.

"A good joke?" Dr. Jamison asks, smiling that smile of his. "Care to tell me?"

"It's nothing," I say. "I'm sorry."

"Do you think you're remembering more things?"

"Yes . . . I think so . . . It's hard to tell . . . I'm still confused sometimes."

"Think about the last few days," Dr. Jamison says. "What triggered a memory for you? Was there an incident, a word, a sound, an image?"

"It was a voice," I say. "I got a phone call."

"Michael," Mother says. "It's Paul."

I take the receiver.

"Yes," I say. "Yes."

"Mike," the voice says. "How are you?"

Mother watches me for a moment, gives an abrupt smile, and then walks out of the kitchen. I hear her climb the stairs.

"Do you remember anything else about Paul besides what he looks like?" Dr. Jamison asks.

I don't answer him right away. I can see Paul's dark hair and the overall shape of his face, but the specifics are blurred. It makes me sad and the more I try to cling to what's left of the memory of his face, the less remains. Perhaps if I hear his voice again, it will all come back.

"I remember . . . ," I say. "Well, it's hard to explain . . ."

"Try," he says and smiles again.

I love Dr. Jamison's smile and I hate it, too. It's beautiful, but sometimes it seems to mock me.

"It isn't any one thing," I say. "It's more like . . . a feeling . . . or something."

How can I explain?

"It's a lot of feelings really," I say.

Dr. Jamison looks at me, doesn't seem ever to stop looking at me. I can't keep up the eye contact and let the garden have my attention for a while.

"Do you know who Paul is?" Dr. Jamison asks.

"When are you coming home, Mike?" Paul's voice asks.

"He's my friend," I tell Dr. Jamison.

"A good friend?" he asks.

"Yes," I say. "I suppose . . . yes, a good friend."

"Your roommate, perhaps?"

I hadn't considered where else I may have lived before and the idea frightens me—as though I'm standing on the edge of a cliff, teetering there. Then the fear is replaced by irritation at Dr. Jamison's questions. He knows the answers, yet he asks me. It's my failure that makes me mad, but my failure seems entirely his fault.

"I don't remember," I say, my voice sharp because I want it to damage. "And you already know the answer."

For just a fraction of a second, Dr. Jamison's smile grows wider.

"You're frustrated," he says. "Why?"

"Because I don't remember," I say, and my face is hot. "Because you know the answers."

Dr. Jamison and I don't speak for a while. I look at my hands. My breathing is rapid. The garden sounds crescendo and disappear into background noise.

"You could just tell me," I say, very quiet. "If you wanted to, you could just tell me everything."

"Do you want to get better?" Dr. Jamison asks and I reply that I do.

"Then it's going to take some work and it's going to be frustrating. I can help you if you want me to," he says.

Again I say, "Yes," but quieter now.

"I'm going to give you a homework assignment," Dr. Jamison says. "We can talk about it on Monday." He pauses as though I'm supposed to speak, but before I can he continues. "I'd like you to interview your family. Think of yourself as a reporter. Come up with three questions, ask each member of your family these questions, start out slow . . . anything you want to know."

"OK," I say in a murmur. The light from the garden grows hot and the air close.

"When is your father coming home?" he asks. "It's soon, isn't it?"

"Yes . . . soon."

Tomorrow? This weekend?

"Is today Wednesday?" I ask.

Dr. Jamison nods. "Wednesday."

"Then, yes . . . soon."

I try to focus on one thing. *Stop smiling.* I push and send the thought out at Dr. Jamison.

His answering machine clicks on and whirs, but we can't hear any talking. Dr. Jamison shifts his gaze for just a moment. His lips go slack and now I can't keep from smiling. I keep most of the smile inside, though. It's a warmth spreading through me, just a quiver showing on my lips.

"How are you doing with the medication?" he asks. "Any side effects?"

"It makes me tired all the time."

He nods. "It does affect some people that way. You might try mild exercise in the midmorning or midafternoon. It's important, though, that you keep taking your medication. It will help keep you calm, help you with those feelings of frustration."

"Mother gives me the pills," I say. "I'd forget otherwise."

Dr. Jamison leans forward, elbows on his knees.

"Let's try to remember some other things," he says. "Lean back. Close your eyes."

Just like last time, a sound grows in volume and eventually drowns out Dr. Jamison's voice. This time, however, I hear music played on a piano—intricate, complicated chords that clash and resolve and clash again. I think I recognize this music, though I can't name it. Abruptly, in midchord, the music stops, then starts again at the beginning.

"Sloppy." I hear a woman's voice. "I want to hear each note. Again."

The music starts over and proceeds slowly, but still I can see nothing.

"Better," the voice says. "Again, please. Now faster. Allegro. And make it flow."

The music stops and when it begins again, it is a different piece—much simpler—and the playing is hesitant and awkward.

"Must you be so mechanical?" the woman's voice asks. "Play the notes, but feel the music."

Then I'm back in Dr. Jamison's office. He sits before me as he did earlier. His eyes smile, but his mouth does not. For several minutes he says nothing and I'm too dazed to speak.

"You've done very well again," he says. A panic builds inside me and before I'm even aware of what's happening, I begin to cry, gasping for breath, then sobbing. Dr. Jamison's expression doesn't change. He turns around and takes a box of tissues from his desk, then hands it to me. I grab one, two, three tissues and blow my nose. The tears stop as abruptly as they started.

"Is this about anything in particular?" Dr. Jamison asks as I continue to sniffle.

I shake my head.

"No," I say and pause to breathe. "I don't know why I did that."

Dr. Jamison nods. "Something you remembered?"

I shake my head again. "It's gone now." I manage a weak smile.

He smiles back.

I know the session is at an end. Dr. Jamison doesn't look at his watch and there is no clock on the wall behind me that he could check. He just seems to know when the hour is over, clued in by some internal psychiatrist's clock.

Stand up, I think and send the thought to him. He stands. I do the same.

It's time to go, I think, and Dr. Jamison says, "Don't forget your homework assignment. We'll talk about it on Monday."

OK, I think, but I don't say a word. I smile instead.

3

Mother writes things on a vinyl calendar in my room. Things for me to remember. She crosses the days off as well, to help me keep track. In the midmorning, while I sit on the bed and watch her, she wipes every surface with a rag, her hands in rubber gloves, an aerosol can always nearby. The first time she did this, I got up to leave the room, but she asked me to stay.

"I'm going downstairs, Mother," I say as she draws an X through yesterday. Before she can say anything, I continue. "Dr. Jamison wants me to exercise every day."

"Oh," she says, dusting the desk, which for several days now has refused to glow. "What sort of exercise are you going to do downstairs?"

I've thought this out and am pleased with myself. "Running in place."

"Running in place," she says. "Sounds invigorating. Maybe we can buy a stationary bike for you. I think they're supposed to be better on your knees. I'll be down in a bit, when I'm done here."

Downstairs I try running in place, but find it difficult to stay put. I begin in the middle of the living room and move inevitably toward the picture window. Then I reposition myself and start the journey again. After two or three times, I tire of running and sit down in the middle of the floor while my breathing returns to normal.

Three questions seem easy. Just three. I should be able to remember three simple questions to ask Karl and Sara and Mother and Dad. Should I ask Karl's wife, whose name I can't remember? Dr. Jamison said to ask my family. My direct family. Is she one of my indirect family?

How old are you? Seems simple enough and it could tell me a lot. Sara looks older, but by how many years? Karl acts older, but is he? If I know my parents' ages then I can calculate how old they were when

I was born, and Amy and Karl, too. Not Amy. I mean Sara. Amy is
Karl's wife.

How do we get along? That too will help me understand more about
us. Of course someone might lie, but whether or not I believe them is
just as revealing.

"Michael," Mother says, coming down the stairs, as if to warn me. I
stay seated in the middle of the floor and twist my body toward her as
she enters the room. She seems surprised. "Oh," she says and stops.
"Did the running tire you?"

"Yes," I say. "Best to start slow."

She smiles, but the smile is forced.

"What would you like to do today?" she asks.

"When is Dad coming home?" I reply and the look on Mother's
face tells me she's heard this question too many times before. She answers politely but with emphasis.

"The day after tomorrow. I wrote it on your calendar. Karl and
Amy and Sara will be here, too."

"That's right," I say and pretend to remember. It's easier to get
along with Mother when she isn't looking worried or sad. If I can't remember, I act as if I can. No harm done and there's always the chance
I will remember later. I can't keep track, though, of what I really
remember and what I just pretend to remember and hope that she
won't either. Sometimes I think she knows, ticking off my failures and
inconsistencies as systematically as she crosses off each day on my vinyl calendar.

Mother leaves the room to put away her rags and aerosol can, but is
still talking to keep me engaged, to keep me remembering.

"Feeling better after your exercise?" she asks, but she doesn't wait
for an answer. "I thought we might look at some photographs," she
says. "Photographs might help you remember."

I know she means well, but I've been avoiding the photographs.
She left some on the table days before—snapshots of Dad and her, of
Sara and Karl and me. But I don't remember the pictures or having
them taken and they lay on the table as evidence of my crime. It isn't
that I've forgotten the places and people, it's that they were never
there to forget. There's an emptiness that fills with anger. The length

of my silence might mean I haven't heard her, yet she doesn't repeat herself. Instead, she comes into the living room holding a large photo album, sits on the sofa, and pauses a moment before slapping the cushion next to her.

I turn my head away, then face her again.

"I'm tired," I say. "Later, OK?"

She opens the album and lays it on her lap, looking at a page, lingering, then closing it as she sighs.

"You could help, you know," she says, her gaze moving up and away as though simply looking at me has become a burden. "Just a little. You could try. It might do you some good."

Sometimes I think the most good would be done if everyone left me alone. *Helping* and *trying* require feeling something specific, understanding connections, wanting to make a difference. I alternate between apathy and bewilderment, between an absence and a chaos. The only connection I understand is between my pretending to remember and Mother pretending everything is normal. The only difference I want to make is the difference between being frustrated and being at peace, being alone.

I move to the sofa, then sit down next to Mother. It's easier this way. Later, if I do well now, she might leave me alone. If I refuse her, she'll just try again. Her expression doesn't change. She's still irritated, but she opens the photo album to the first pages and moves it so it sits half in my lap and half in hers. Then she waits while I study the pictures.

Some of the older photos show three children arranged in front of a house or a fence or a car. Sometimes a much younger version of Mother joins the group—her face is smooth and carefully made up and her thick black hair is curled under, just above her shoulders. She wears a full-length coat and a small round hat that seems to float above her head on a cushion of that hair. The children, I know, are Karl and Sara and me. I'm the youngest, always holding on to someone—Karl's hand, Mother's dress, Sara's arm. In every picture, I'm pouting, frowning, scowling at the camera and, it seems, at Dad. He's absent from these photos and must, I assume, be the one recording the whole thing, choosing which fraction of time to capture. Was I really scowling all the time, or did Dad always manage to catch me just as my infant patience ran out?

Karl looks just a little older than me but is smiling. He stands on his own, his hair shiny and neatly slicked to his head. His eyes are full of energy and mischief, as though he would break into a cartwheel as soon as the camera lens closed. Sara poses. She's obviously older than Karl and me, is still just a little girl, but one who seems to understand what the camera sees. Unlike Karl, who smiles at the camera as if it were a friend waving hello, Sara is a little fashion model, playing to the camera with a crooked smile, a calculated tilt of her head and a toss of her curly hair.

I nod a few times while I look at the photos, not because I recognize any of them, but because they seem to confirm what I've seen of Mother and Karl and Sara already. People don't change, I guess, not really. The photos also fit what I know about myself so far—frustrated and helpless. Have I always been like this? These photos can't say, but maybe others can.

"Of course, you don't remember having these taken," Mother says, her voice no longer sounding irritated. "But you remember seeing them before, don't you?"

I nod a few more times. It's what she wants. She turns the page.

Several of the photographs are tinted bluish lavender by time and chemicals. Some of them have other adults and children in them, relations and friends I don't recognize. In one of them, though, a handsome man stands leaning against a road sign that reads

> **Piano**
> **Elevation 207**
> **Population 106**

For a moment I think it's Karl, but then realize it's Dad when he was around the age Karl is now. I touch the photo and say, "Piano," then laugh.

"You remember that, don't you?" Mother says.

"It's the name of a town," I say, and though I don't remember the photo or the place where it was taken, I get the joke and laugh again.

"I swear it was the first word you recognized in print. When you saw that sign you started to shout and we had to turn the car around to see what all the fuss was about. Remember?"

I nod again. "Piano, piano, piano," I shout in a singsong voice, then immediately wonder if I've gone too far in my effort to convince Mother. The chant comes without my thinking about it. Perhaps I do remember, but can I say I remember if there's no tingle of recognition, if only my vocal chords recall?

Mother laughs now too.

On the remainder of the photo album's pages, I see my family age in sometimes subtle and sometimes dramatic leaps. In groups of five or three or four or one, they and I grow more like the family I find myself among. They are a photogenic bunch, except for me. In one photograph, Karl and I look around sixteen or seventeen. It's one of the rare pictures in which I'm smiling. Karl has his arm draped around my neck and my head is cocked to one side and resting on his shoulder. We look as though we've just finished rolling down a hillside or wrestling in the grass. It's such a sweet photograph and I'm oddly jealous of the boy in the picture—the boy who looks like me.

"Can I bring this upstairs?" I ask Mother. "This picture. Maybe frame it."

She looks confused.

"Well," she says. "Well, of course. And . . . and maybe this family portrait, too." She points to a more recent photo. The family is posed, in ties and shirts and nice dresses, in front of a photographer's backdrop. Everyone smiles, of course, except me. I don't care for the photo, don't enjoy looking at it in the same way I enjoy looking at the other.

"Sure," I say. "Sure, both of them . . . I'll put both of them in my room."

Later, upstairs, I lie on my bed and stare at the two pictures. At first I'm conscious of looking. I take in little details—a tear in the shoulder of Karl's T-shirt, the glazed look in Sara's eyes that contrasts her poised smile, Mother's frilly dress which seems unlike anything I've seen her wear—but then I realize I'm not focusing anymore, not even aware of what I'm staring at. My mind has drifted away, but I'll call it back when I need it. Not now, though. I let my thoughts go and I stare.

Time passes. That's the only thing I'm sure of.

How old are you? I ask, but I don't make a sound. I know I have to repeat the questions so they will stay in my brain, imprint themselves. This is how I remember.

"Try practicing facts, things you know," Dr. Jamison said to me. "Repeat them to yourself, as if you were an actor preparing for a play. Telephone numbers, people's names. Repeat them to yourself enough times and they'll be second nature. It's the way people get good at remembering names. Think of it as an exercise and don't take it too seriously if you can't remember everything. You'll get better at it eventually."

I'm twenty-nine, I think. *How do we get along?*

"I didn't think they'd really go through with it," Karl said to me and I don't believe him. I look at the photograph of us and I can see in my smile that I believed him once. When I was fifteen or sixteen, I believed everything he told me. Something changed or maybe it was my brain being scrambled. Maybe nothing has changed at all and I'll be able to smile again the way I'm smiling in the photo. Maybe we get along just fine, Karl and I. Maybe we're best friends.

Do we share a secret? I shouldn't expect the truth. One of them may be a hit-and-run driver. One of them may have broken a china plate while playing with me and helped glue it back together so no one else would know.

Everything starts to make sense, but in a way I can't pin down. The thread of my argument becomes visible, weaving in and out, connecting thoughts that once seemed rambling and chaotic. Is this being lucid? It's pleasant but seems difficult to maintain. In fact, it's gone when I recognize it, which doesn't upset me as much as I think it should.

I keep staring at the photographs. My eyelids close and after a few attempts at keeping them open, I lay my head down on the pillow and sleep.

Sasha visits me. I thought he'd left forever, that he couldn't or wouldn't appear in the house, but he sits in the desk chair, his legs crossed, his thin wrists emerging from enormous starched cuffs, looking a bit like a boy wearing his father's suit.

"I'm not actually here, of course," he says. "You're asleep. You're dreaming."

"So you're gone, then?" I ask.

"*Alors,* what I say in your dream isn't important. What I say now could be whatever you had for dinner."

"Not if you're what you say you are."

"If you wish," Sasha says. "It remains your dream . . ." He fidgets in the chair, smoothes his waistcoat.

"Will I see you again when I'm awake?" I ask. "Or have you finished with me?"

"Finished," he says, "implies an end. You know there is no end, no beginning. I don't understand the question and so I can't answer it. It doesn't make any sense to me. Haven't we gone over this before?"

"Everything makes sense to you. You've become God, remember?"

"Being at home has made you petulant, Michael. I preferred you in the hospital."

"I was drugged and incoherent."

"And so could listen and learn. Sometimes that is what it takes," Sasha says and tosses his head, brushes back his hair. His oversized, waxed mustache looks ludicrous but fascinates me. "If you remember, Michael, I am the Spirit. I am Creativity. I don't deal in past, present, or future. Everything just is."

"How convenient," I say.

Sasha shrugs, his expression infuriatingly calm. "Whatever you say, Michael. It is your dream."

"I want you to go away." Even before the words are out, I regret what I've said. Sasha nods and begins to grow transparent.

"Wait," I say.

Sasha has become a faint slide projected before me on an invisible screen. He continues to smile. Just before he vanishes, I hear him whisper, "Adieu."

I wake up and it's morning. The first things I see are the photographs on the nightstand. There is a moment of fuzziness, but when it passes I know where I am and who I am and who the people in the photograph are. I recognize my room and know Mother is downstairs. I can picture the living room, the kitchen, the yard, and I can see the calendar with its Xs across each preceding day. I know it's Thursday. I know Dad will be home tomorrow.

I'm cured. I lie in bed and I play a little game, thinking back over the days since I came home, remembering conversations, visits with Dr. Jamison, dinner with Karl and Sara and Amy, driving home from the hospital, my confusions, my frustrations. I remember and remember and remember and the act of remembering becomes a physical sensation, like drinking water to quench a thirst. I try to go back farther in time, to my stay in the hospital and before that, but no images come. It doesn't bother me really because I'm better. Before the hospital, I know, things were very wrong. I'm fixed now and if that means I have a blank space before I came home, I'm willing to accept that. I'm willing to pay for my happiness with a chunk of forgotten time.

The clock says 7:00 and the light is starting to glow behind the window shades.

In the kitchen, Mother's sitting at the table, drinking a cup of coffee. She's surprised I'm awake so early, sputtering her "Good morning" and jumping up to get me a glass of orange juice.

"I can get it myself, Mother," I say. "Just relax for a bit. Finish your coffee."

My confidence makes her smile.

"You seem better," she says.

"I feel pretty good." I get a glass, open the refrigerator, pour myself some juice, then sit down across from her. "Not so fuzzy." I smile without even trying. "Not so tired." For a moment, everything is normal. The sunlight gives the kitchen a yellowish look, one full of possibilities and beginnings.

"Hungry?" she asks and I shake my head, still smiling.

"I'll just make myself some toast."

Then my moment of confidence is gone. I start to wonder if my incessant smiling looks crazy. The act of making toast has to be broken into parts so I can picture what my movements will be. I take a sip of the orange juice and all my doubts disappear. Everything seems normal again, even that flash of the old craziness seems in keeping with the kitchen, the light, the juice, and Mother's coffee. It won't be so bad.

"Can I ask you some questions?" I say.

"Questions?" she repeats and keeps smiling, as though I'm some interesting stranger flirting with her. "What kind of questions?"

"Just some questions. Some things I don't remember. Dr. Jamison thinks it will help me if I start asking more questions."

"There's a lot you don't remember, isn't there?" she asks, and then the words come out in a rush. "It's been so difficult to talk to you about it." She stops, her look one of astonishment and relief, and sips some of her coffee. We face each other for a while, smiles pasted on, then Mother says, "Ask me whatever you want, whatever will help."

I have three questions. I've practiced these questions to myself, repeated them in my head, and now, when the time comes to ask them, I wonder how appropriate they are. Faced with another person who will take the questions in, process them, and return them to me transformed, I'm shy.

"I need some paper," I say, "and a pen. Dr. Jamison wants me to write things down."

"Of course," she says, pushing away from the table and opening a drawer. A pad and a pencil appear before me. I pick up the pencil, clear my throat. Mother looks at me and nods. She's sitting again.

"OK," I say. *How old are you?* I write on the pad. "So, the first question . . . OK, the first question is pretty easy . . ."

"Whatever is going to help," Mother says.

"How old are you?" Once the question is out, I'm embarrassed. I look at the pad, hold the pencil ready to record her answer, but for a while she says nothing.

"You're right. It's quite an easy question. I'm . . . sixty-two. Sixty-two. I was thirty-three when you were born. You're twenty-nine."

I nod. "Twenty-nine."

I write sixty-two on the pad and prepare for the next question. *How do we get along?* I print.

There is an uncomfortable silence. "What else?" she asks.

"OK, well . . . how do we get along?" Again I look at the pad and wait.

"Do you mean now or . . . before?"

"Before . . . I mean before." And I write the word *before* above the question.

"Well," she says and takes a deep breath. "Well, Michael, to tell the truth . . . you were very difficult to get along with." She looks at me, searching for some hint of a reaction in my face. Since I don't remember *before,* I'll believe her. I was difficult. Why else would they give me the treatment?

"You were angry," she says. "It's never easy to get along with someone who's angry so much of the time."

I nod. What made me so angry? I wonder, but it's not one of my questions and Dr. Jamison said to take it slowly at first. I write down *Difficult. Angry a lot. Why?* The *Why?* is for later.

"I think we got along well when you were a child," Mother says. "You were very quiet, very sweet, but around junior high school you started to change—still quiet, but so moody. Karl was the only one who could get you out of your moods. I thought it was just adolescence, but you never grew out of it that I could see. Then you went away to college and God knows what happened there. You just seemed to get angrier and moodier. I never figured out how to get along with you as an adult." She stares at her coffee cup, swirls the leftover liquid around, and then looks up at me with a twisted little smile. "That's a rather sad statement, isn't it?"

I smile back and raise my eyebrows in sympathy. It is a sad statement, I suppose. I certainly wouldn't know how to get along with someone that angry or moody either. It's difficult to imagine me as Mother describes. Why can't I sustain that kind of anger anymore? Is it the pills? On the pad, I write *Sustained anger,* then cross out the word *anger* and write above it *feeling.*

"We're being awfully serious for so early in the day," Mother says as she gets up and pours herself more coffee. She begins preparing some toast as well. "Are you sure you don't want some eggs or cereal?"

"Just toast, really," I say.

"What else?" she asks.

"Just toast, Mother."

"I know that, Michael. What else do you want to ask me?"

I look down at the pad, but I haven't written down the third question. *How old are you? How do we get along?* I swear I wrote the third question down, but now I can't remember what it is.

"I think that's enough for right now," I say. "Dr. Jamison wants me to start slowly."

Mother gets the butter out of the refrigerator and looks at the toaster, which grows hotter. I can see the top of red coils from where I sit.

"What do you want to do today?" she asks, just as the toaster pings and two slices of toast pop up.

In my room, the light begins to fade and though it's still late afternoon, I know it's also winter and night falls early. I wait as long as I can, lying on my bed and watching the shadows crawl across my room, seeing the air grow fuzzy and granular like an out-of-focus photograph. It's peaceful. There's a sadness in it as well, but it's comfortable sadness, one that reassures me.

Electric light tears through the room, destroying the shadows.

"What are you doing lying in the dark?" Mother asks. There is a split second before I close my eyes. I see her standing at the door, her hand still on the light switch, but cupped, as if she holds a small object. In her other hand is a glass of water.

I have to close my eyes. There's a pain in my head and I place my arm over my face to block out more of the light.

"Nothing," I say.

"Were you sleeping?" she asks. "Time for your pills."

"No. I was just thinking."

I can hear her set the glass on my desk and stand near the bed. I know she's holding my pills out to me, so I extend my hand to accept them. She gives them to me and I can feel them in my palm as I sit up and, with my eyes still shut, hold out my other hand for the glass.

The day has gone by quickly and mysteriously. Dinner will be ready soon and although I can remember what I did throughout the day, what I did was so uneventful and generic that the entire day seems not to have existed at all. After the morning conversation with Mother, I watched her cleaning, then I napped on the sofa in the basement where she could watch me as she painted. I turned on the television in the afternoon. Mother tolerated this as long as I kept the volume low and she wasn't in the family room. I watched the television and got tired, so I ran in place.

The programs on the television make me tired, I think. It isn't the pills after all. The television programs mesmerize me and take my strength away. I wish I could prove it, run an experiment to see if I'm just as tired when I don't watch television, but the process for doing this seems too complicated. I can't even recall if I'm the one who turned off the television or if Mother did it because I fell asleep. The running didn't seem to help much, but the fact that I could get myself to stand up and then run in place is good. Maybe it isn't the television programs. Maybe it's the pills after all.

The television programs are mostly stories that have many characters related to or connected with other characters. These stories are broken up by commercials and although I know which are the programs and which are the commercials, I can't always be sure when one program ends and the next starts. The events happening on the programs are important. The people are serious and the music tells me to pay attention, tells me how I'm supposed to react. The music's instructions register with me, but I can't do as I'm told. All I can do is observe.

The people in the television blend from one program to the next and the commercials shout at me. I turn the volume down only to turn it up again when the programs come back on. I keep my hand on the volume button, pointing the remote control at the television until my arm becomes tired and I have to rest it on the sofa.

At some point during the day, I remembered the third question I meant to ask Mother and wrote it down on the piece of paper. *Do we share any secrets?* It occurred to me that keeping a separate sheet for each interviewee would make things more organized. Across the top of the first page, I wrote MOTHER and underlined the word. I tore it off the pad and wrote SARA across the top of the next one. I copied the three questions and left a lot of space between them so I can take notes. I repeated this procedure twice more for DAD and KARL.

So now, as I sit in my room and wait for Mother to call me to dinner, I shuffle the papers, putting KARL first, then DAD, then changing my mind and putting MOTHER on top, reasoning that my interview with her was unfinished and therefore of higher priority. I read the notes I took, which amount to a few words: *Difficult. Angry a lot. Why? Sustained feelings.* Even in conjunction with the questions and with what I remember from our conversation this morning, the notes seem cryptic. At the time I wrote them they were important, but now I look at them for help, for meaning, and the words refuse to give up any secrets.

"Michael," Mother calls. "Dinner."

"I finished the painting today," Mother says. She eats her salad slowly, impaling bits of lettuce and shaved carrots on her fork. She holds the fork with the prongs facing down and the stem fitting into the palm of her left hand. I imitate the way she holds her silverware, but I'm not as adept at keeping the salad on the fork. Bits of my salad fall onto the table without a sound as Mother watches but doesn't comment.

"That's good," I say. "Will you sell it?"

She chews her salad, smiles, and gives a little shrug.

"We'll see." Mother never speaks until she finishes chewing her food. She dabs her mouth with her napkin. "Come downstairs after dinner and tell me what you think."

What do I think of Mother's paintings? They all seem so similar—masses of stars and cosmic gas clouds, occasionally some small planets with rings or swirling, colorful atmospheres. Perhaps it's the sameness of the pictures that makes people want to buy them. The buyers know what to expect, but they also know each painting is unique. "The touch of red in that gas cloud really gives the picture focus," I could say. Or "That blank area just off center seems ominous." How am I coming up with this stuff? I'm not sure if I'm remembering past comments or just inventing them on the spot. Either way, I'm glad.

"Sure," I say, buoyed by my mental state. "Who better to comment on space than someone so spacey?"

Mother's face goes slack and her fork stops midway to her mouth.

"Don't be ridiculous," she says, her lips tight. "You're doing very well."

"Just a joke, Mother."

"I don't find it amusing, Michael. It just isn't something to make light of."

The fork continues its trajectory. Mother chews her salad and looks down at her plate, as if planning her next bite.

"I was joking, Mother," I say, bewildered by her reaction.

She concentrates on her salad, shaking her head.

"I didn't mean anything by it."

"Can we change the subject, please?" she asks.

"You're mad now. I don't understand why you're mad."

She sets down her fork.

"I'm angry, Michael. Angry, not mad. Mad means crazy."

"But what are you angry about? You're acting like I insulted you."

"You insulted yourself," she says. "You dismissed the seriousness of your situation with a flip remark. It's your self-deprecating humor that makes me so angry. It makes me wonder how well you understand what's happened to you."

"Obviously not well enough."

Mother doesn't say anything for a moment. She just watches me. I imagine she can hear my heart pounding.

Her expression changes from stony to heartbreaking. It's her eyes. They've lost their look of squinting reproach and are now wider, surprised and resigned at the same time. The silence rings.

"My God, you haven't changed a bit, have you?" she says at last, but it isn't a question at all. "I really shouldn't be surprised, I suppose, but I'd hoped . . ." For a moment, I think I see tears forming in her eyes, and a hollow ache settles in my stomach. I can't think of anything to say to her. She pushes her chair away from the table. "Just set your dishes in the sink when you're through," she says and walks out of the dining room. "I'll clean up later." I hear her ascend the stairs, stumbling once on the way up.

In the morning, I pretend I don't remember eating dinner or having an argument. I ask Mother if she's finished her painting yet and if I can see it. At first she looks surprised and a little angry, but then she finally understands there may be an advantage to my memory lapses. She acts as though last night hadn't happened. But it has happened. Nothing's the same.

"Your father will be home tonight," Mother says. We're in the living room—Mother dusting and straightening, me just sitting on the sofa.

"Yes," I say. "I saw it on the calendar. Can I help with anything? Cleaning? Shopping?"

"No, no. Everything's under control."

The telephone rings and, maybe because I'm startled, I jump off the sofa and am standing. "I'll get it," I say. I walk through the dining room and into the kitchen. I know what to do now—pick up the handset and speak into the receiver.

"Hello," I say.

"Hello, Mike," a man's voice says. It sounds familiar, and then I know.

"Paul," I say, excited. "Hello. How are you?"

"I miss you so much," he says. "But other than that, I'm doing OK."

"Michael," Mother calls. "Who is it?"

"It's for me," I shout and my tone brings her into the kitchen to see for herself.

"Where are you?" I ask, turning my back to Mother.

"At home. In the apartment." His words bring up no pictures for me. There are so many questions I want to ask, but I'm afraid of scaring him and I'm self-conscious with Mother around. Even the simplest question seems private. Paul's voice is just above a whisper and it's as though we're talking in secret, like lovers meeting clandestinely. I haven't heard Mother leave the room, but I don't feel her behind me. Her sensation is everywhere in the house, though. She listens and watches, as protective and pervasive as a fog.

"I wish you were here right now," Paul says.

"I'd like that."

There is silence between us for a moment, then Paul says, "Look, I'm sorry about the things I said before. You needed help. I let you down."

"Paul," I say.

"And this is what happens."

"It's not your fault."

He laughs, though it's a sad sound. "It's just as well you don't remember."

There is another pause, then Paul says nervously, "You remember me, don't you?"

"Yes," I tell him, picturing the shadowy man I associate with his voice.

"And our apartment?"

I think the word *yes* because I don't want to hurt him, but no sound comes out of my throat.

"Jesus, Mike," Paul says.

"Things come back to me all the time. Dr. Jamison says it will all come back eventually."

"Of course it will. I love you. Just don't forget that."

"I won't." I must have loved him, too, but I don't think I can say those words back. Not yet. I look into the dining and living rooms. Mother is gone. "When will I see you?" I ask. "Are you nearby?"

"Oh, God," is all he says.

"Dad's coming home tonight. We'll all be here. Maybe you can come, too."

"Mike, if I came for you, would you leave with me? Would you come back home?"

His words shock and thrill me. I hear a soft click on the phone line.

"Hello," Paul says. "Mike, are you there?"

Mother is listening. I know it. The only thing I can do is hang up without speaking. It's an act of cowardice or an act of survival. Maybe both. My hand is still on the telephone receiver when Mother comes into the kitchen again.

"Was it Paul?" she asks.

Her seeming nonchalance is impressive. She puts my pills on the counter and goes to the sink to fill a glass of water.

"Yes."

"Are you all right, Michael?" She hands me the glass and my pills, but I don't take them from her. "Did Paul upset you?"

"No."

"Take your pills," she says, and I do as she tells me. I swallow the pills and drink the entire glass of water. Mother stares at me. "He's calling here too often," she says. "You're not ready to talk to your friends yet. Look at you. I think I'll answer the phone from now on."

"I'm fine."

"Do you want to get better?" Mother asks.

"Of course."

"Then you need to listen to Dr. Jamison and you need to listen to me. Paul is not your doctor. He just confuses you."

I'm not the same after talking to Paul, it's true. So much of my life is gone and I'm afraid it won't come back, but maybe I'm better off not knowing. Mother said I was always angry and difficult before all this happened. I don't want to go back to that. I should be able to control that now.

"Why don't you lie down?" Mother says. "Tonight's a big night."

When I wake, it will be afternoon and there will be dinner to prepare and the big event to anticipate—Dad's coming home. The beginning of something. I have to be on my best behavior—responsive, alert, coherent—and I have to seem normal. Not fully normal. That would be too much to pull off. On the road to recovery. Favorably improved.

"I'll come and wake you when it's time for your pills again," Mother says. "Your father should be getting in around six-thirty. Sara is supposed to be here at five. I expect Karl and Amy at six." She takes my hand off the telephone receiver and gently pushes me out of the kitchen. "You go rest. Everything's under control."

I sleep for a while, but then I'm wide awake and want to make sure I have my questions right. I take my prepared pages from the desk drawer, once again arranging and rearranging them, trying to decide the order. Then this act begins to disturb me. I wonder if it's obsessive, if the act of moving these papers around has any rational purpose besides keeping my hands busy while I blank out. Except I'm not blanking out at all. I'm wondering if I'm obsessing.

I hear Sara arrive downstairs and enter the house, closing the door with a thud and calling out, "It's me. I'm late. Traffic sucked." The sound of her retreats into the house, toward the kitchen. I can hear that she and Mother are talking, but it comes to me as mumbling, the words indistinguishable from one another and occasionally punctuated by the sound of furniture being moved.

It occurs to me that I might just ask Sara why she seems so disgusted with me, but I'm afraid the answer and my reaction could make things worse. With Mother, I can pretend to remember and she wants to believe me so much that she does. I don't think it would be the same with Sara. She dislikes and distrusts me. Similarly, if I didn't remember and said so, she might think I was lying to avoid responsibility, taking the easy way out. I have to skip her for the time being. Dr. Jamison will understand. He'll understand that she's too angry and I'm not ready.

It's stupid, though. Here's a woman I don't remember, yet I'm afraid of how she'll react—as if this whole thing is my fault, as if I'm to blame for not remembering and for whatever happened. I have no evidence for this, yet I have no evidence to tell me otherwise. I want straightforward answers to simple questions, but I know better than to think twenty-eight years of my life can be summed up so easily. Twenty-nine years, I mean. I'm twenty-nine.

This whole exercise is a waste of time. If the point is getting me to remember, my interview with Mother didn't help me there. If the point is to bring me closer to my family, that too seems doomed. I feel nothing for these people except a vague sense of discomfort—as though I've been plucked from some land of forgetting and delivered to a family at random. Perhaps this whole thing was arranged—photos doctored, official documents forged, money changing hands in high places. It's ludicrous, I know. None of this seems right. Everything seems staged. I'm the actor in the midst of some nightmare where everyone but me knows the plot and their parts. I struggle along, improvising, blowing my lines, but careful not to break character so I won't be sent back to the world of the tranquilizing light and scrambled brains.

I look at the vinyl calendar on the wall. I look at the desk that doesn't glow, at the windows, at the pictures on the nightstand. I sit on the bed and I look and look and look. The hands on the clock are moving, but I can't see them move. The walls of the bedroom are decaying, but none of that is visible. I'm growing less distinct in the failing light, my hands, my legs losing definition and decomposing into molecules that spread into the very air around me—yet if I move, if I turn on the lights, everything returns to normal. Nothing will be different except the positions of the clock's hands.

Downstairs, Mother and Sara are busy cooking, cleaning, planning. Everyone will be here tonight. Everyone who matters.

I look at the pictures on the nightstand again. The man in the family photo is me, the boy in the photo with Karl less obviously so. I want to be able to smile as that boy is smiling. I just want to smile and not think about the act of smiling.

Downstairs, they're planning.

What would they say, those planners downstairs, if they knew that the only person I remember doesn't even live here? My memory of Paul is vague, though, and I wonder—where did we live? How long ago? Where is he now? And yet am I really remembering Paul or recollecting an emotion between comfort and excitement, between familiarity and fear, and attaching it to a face I see in my mind?

At the end of the hall, Mother is coming up the stairs with my pills and a glass of water. I can tell by the sound of her footsteps. To my surprise, though, it's Sara who enters my room.

"Are you asleep?" she asks. "It's dark in here." She stops near the door as if waiting for me to invite her in. I sit up in bed.

"No. I'm awake."

"Mother says to take your pills." She doesn't move, just stands there holding the glass of water out to me.

"Sure. Come on in."

She turns on the light suddenly and I'm not prepared. I wince, cover my eyes.

"Sorry," she says without much sincerity. I hear her move closer and wait for the sound of the glass being set on the nightstand. There's silence for too long, so I open my eyes. Sara's in the same position as before, the glass still in her hand, but she's closer to me, like a statue picked up at the door and set down by my bed.

I hold out my hand. She gives me the glass of water, the pills.

"Thanks," I say.

She continues to stand there, looking at me.

"Mom says I'm supposed to make sure you take those." She doesn't smirk, but I can tell she wants to, that only a warning from Mother is holding her back.

In rapid succession, I pop the pills into my mouth, drink the water in two gulps, and open my mouth wide so she can see I've swallowed. There's a touch of nastiness in the gesture to be sure.

"Mission accomplished," Sara says flatly. "Maybe tonight you won't drool." She turns to leave.

"Sara," I say. Seeing her here, listening to her disdain, I'm suddenly a little boy again, standing near a ride at a carnival. I hear the mechanical music and smell grease frying.

"I do remember something," I say. "I was five or six and you slapped me, very hard, for looking stupid. That's what you said: 'You look stupid.' You slapped me right after I got off the tilt-a-whirl. Do you remember that?" She stands where she is but turns and doesn't face me.

"Don't be ridiculous." She says the words as if she's holding each at arm's length like so many dirty rags, then she runs her fingers through her thick, curly hair.

"Forget it," I say. Perhaps she never slapped me. Another false memory. Another short circuit. I want her out of the room now. "Tell Mother I'll be down in a bit."

Sara's face remains calm, but her hands curl into fists as she places them on her hips.

"It's obvious that a few zaps to your brain haven't changed you at all." Her voice becomes very low and sharp. She doesn't look at me. "You're still a spoiled little shit that we all have to tiptoe around. 'Don't bother Michael. Be careful with Michael. You know what Michael's like.' Oh, I know what he's like and I'm sick of playing along." She turns and walks out.

I have a confounding sense of freedom now that the room is empty. Sara's anger and bitterness leave with her. The space between what I'm experiencing and what is happening around me opens up and reveals its span. I'm cut off from the rest of the house, peaceful, unconcerned, basking in the weird realization that nothing anyone says or does to me matters because the context has been erased. It seems so simple, so obvious, but until now this calm eluded me. I'm ready for whatever happens tonight—for Dad, for Karl, for all of it. At the same time, I'm in no hurry to go downstairs because this calm, this peace, doesn't include obligations or thoughts of expectations. I *am* a spoiled little shit. At this moment that's all I am; it's my label, my whole existence. I don't want to get out of bed. I can't. It seems to suit me, this shitdom of mine. Maybe it's the pills. Maybe this sense of control is only an illusion, the results of the chemicals in my bloodstream blocking electric impulses or some hormone. Should it matter if it's real or the pills? Does it?

I think of Paul. I close my eyes and concentrate on what I remember. In this calmness, there seems an ease in recollection. I just close my eyes and think of him. I think of his comfortable stockiness. At first his face is blank, like a mannequin's, but slowly his features fill in—his face is round, his hair is thick, wiry, and dark. Brown eyes, very large and playful. His eyebrows almost meet, which keeps his playfulness in check, giving him a serious look even when he smiles. This is the image I see when I hear his voice. I remember him but have little sense of satisfaction. I remember specifics but can't remember him in context.

Downstairs, I hear the front door open, hear voices raised in greeting—female voices mostly, but Karl's as well. The door closes and the voices retreat into the house.

Karl, I think. I form his name in my mind and push it out. Perhaps he's too far away to receive me. *Karl.*

Another thought disrupts my calm, then is gone, like a moment of static breaking into a telephone call. I can't be sure where the thought comes from—is it from me or from Karl? The rogue thought pierces my calm, passes right through it, and it bursts. My heart beats faster. I can't deny the odd sensation that there is no longer this strict distinction between the inside and outside of my head. My thoughts have shape, texture, and the capacity for movement like the furniture in my room. Instead of talking, instead of pushing air out through my mouth and shaping it, I'm pushing thoughts out through the pores of my skin. Is it electrical? Chemical?

I push. *Karl.*

Someone is walking up the stairs.

Karl.

Someone is walking down the hall, stopping outside the door.

Come in. I push.

Someone knocks.

I push out air. "Yes?" I say.

Mother opens the door but doesn't enter.

"Why don't you come downstairs?" she asks. "Karl and Amy are here."

"OK." I blink and the blink makes a sound. Mother doesn't notice, so I blink again and again I hear the noise of the blink, like a camera shutter clicking. Mother frowns.

"I have no idea what you told Sara," she says, "but she's in one of her moods again." Mother sighs. "It looks like nothing's changed between you two. It's going to be a long evening."

"She was already mad when she came in here." I blink a few more times. Click click click.

"You mean she was already angry," Mother says. "Why are you blinking?"

Amy is helping Mother in the kitchen while Karl sits in the living room reading a newspaper. I come down the stairs quietly and can observe him before he realizes I'm here. Watching him like this, I imagine there's a spell on him and if I gaze too long he will vanish. His jaw, smooth and shaven but tinged blue by his heavy beard, twitches slightly as he reads. His head is down, his attention on the newspaper, so I can't see his eyes. I look at his lips, how damp and pink they seem.

He sees me.

"Hey, you," he says. "How long have you been watching me?" His tone is joking, but I can hear another meaning beneath the words. His eyes tell me I'm imagining things. I blink and the movement makes my heart beat faster. I must be blushing. My face is hot.

"I wasn't watching you," I say and hide another meaning beneath my words. *I was watching your lips. Now I'm regarding the curve of your throat.*

"Hello, Mike," Amy says. She comes into the living room without a sound, but her presence speaks to me as clearly as her words. Karl smiles and for a moment I'm sure he's heard my thoughts. There's nothing to do but descend the stairs, walk into the living room, sit down, wait for Dad and dinner, and continue progressing in time and space.

"Sara went to pick up Dad at the airport," Karl says.

"He won't be hungry at all," Mother says from the kitchen. "He'll just pick at his dinner." She speaks loudly to be heard across the dining room between us.

"Hey, Mom, *we're* hungry," Karl calls back. "Forget about him!"

Amy laughs as if she's part of this. It's her family, I think. It isn't mine at all. It's hers. She's holding a blue dish towel. She wipes her hands on it and goes back into the kitchen, leaving Karl and me alone again. I'm sitting on the sofa across from him. We look at each other, not speaking. We smile instead. There are lots of smiles in this house. They fill those spaces between words.

"When's Dad supposed to be here?" I ask Karl, but Mother answers instead, though she couldn't have heard me.

"Your father should be home any minute now," she says, "but you never know."

"I don't know if you remember how he is about dinner," Karl says. "Mom has to time it so the food is ready as soon as he gets home. He can't stand waiting. One of his little eccentricities."

I don't remember, of course, but Karl's manner, his politeness in explanation, is comforting. Or perhaps it's just his even skin tone and the elegant curve of his nose that puts me more at ease.

"What are the other ones?" I ask.

Karl's expression shifts. A suggestion of concern comes across his brow, then vanishes.

"Too many to list," he says, trying to make it a joke, then lowering his voice. "Don't you remember anything about him?"

"I've seen his picture." I haven't answered Karl's question, not really, but either he thinks I did or he decides not to pursue it. He nods. There is an uncomfortable pause, then he looks down at the newspaper again.

"I have a photograph of us," I say. The words come out in a desperate blurt, which I try to soften with clipped explanations. "Upstairs. In my room. From when we were kids."

Karl looks up and his smile this time sends a sharp and beautiful pain through me. He hasn't looked this way before. My throat tightens.

"We . . . look so . . . happy," I say, and my voice stops. I have to look away, toward the dining room. I don't understand what's come over me and I wait for it to pass. Within seconds, this desolate excitement is gone and replaced by a horrible stillness.

"What's Mother making for dinner?" I ask. I'm able to look at Karl again and see that whatever he felt is gone as well. None of us can sustain our emotions, it seems. We're a family all right. If I weren't so calm, I'd make a run for the front door and never look back. The last thing I want right now is food. The thought of chewing and swallowing is unappealing. The smells from the kitchen hover. I take them in, but I can't relish them.

"It smells like garlic," Karl says, sniffing. "And tomatoes . . . it must be her authentic Dutch/German lasagna." He says it like it's a joke, so I laugh a little. "What's for dinner, Mom?" Karl shouts.

She comes into the living room, wiping her hands on a towel. "Lasagna," she says. "Garlic bread and salad. Your father's favorite and his specific request for tonight."

"Homecoming lasagna," Karl says, looking at me conspiratorially.

Mother gives us a good-natured nod. "How are you feeling, Michael?"

"Fine." Nothing either of them said in the last minute means much to me. I should care. I don't. I should be frustrated. I'm not. Mother studies me for a moment.

"Homecoming lasagna," Karl says again.

"Well, it's a special occasion. We're all here together and you're back with us, Michael. That makes it very special. Why don't you change into some nice clothes . . . dress for dinner?" She nods at Karl. "Karl can help you. You've got some time to freshen up, wash your face, comb your hair." There's a chirping brightness in her voice.

"She thinks you look like a bum," Karl says and Mother glares at him.

"That's not what I meant, Karl."

"Just kidding, Mom," he says. "Come on, Mike, let's spruce you up before Dad gets home." Karl stands and holds out his hand to me. I take it. He pulls me to my feet and we leave the room, Karl leading. Our hands still clasped, we ascend the stairs. The warmth of his palm meets mine and where we touch a pulsating heat grows. I feel so childish, so protected. Our skin seems joined. My powerlessness sends a shiver from our point of contact into my arm, across my shoulders, and down my back. Karl squeezes my hand. Before I can return the gesture, we reach the top of the stairs and he releases me. I'm not prepared, stumble backward. Karl catches me.

"Still a little shaky, huh?" he asks, his arm around me, supporting me as we walk down the hallway. I don't need his help now, but his arm feels good so I do nothing to let him know I'm fine. I can hear Sara telling me what a spoiled little shit I am.

In my room, Karl sits me on the chair at the desk and slides the closet door open.

"Not much to choose from," he says, moving aside shirts and pants on hangers. "Just what you brought and all these old clothes." He holds out a denim shirt much too small for me. It has checkered material forming a yoke over the shoulders. "You could put this on and see if Dad notices."

"It won't fit."

He looks at me and the right side of his mouth moves upward in a smirk. "You *have* forgotten a lot, haven't you? Dad's pretty self-absorbed. No, wait, let's just say he's very selective about his attention to mundane details." It's the first time I've heard Karl make a sarcastic remark. For a moment, the tone of his voice, the way he stands, even the minute movements of his face all remind me of Sara. I wonder if the same thing happens to me, if it's a family trait, some genetic code for the physical expression of contempt and sarcasm. It all fades and the even-tempered, gentlemanly Karl is back.

"He's a great artist," he says, turning to the closet. "I guess we've all learned to accept his idiosyncrasies."

Karl moves several more shirts.

"He plays the piano, doesn't he?" I ask. I almost say *Dad* instead of *he,* but the word seems odd and stays in my throat. "How come there's no piano in the house?"

"He comes home to get away from all that," Karl says, then holds out another shirt to me, a white one with a button-down collar. "This should work with anything, don't you think?"

I nod and stand up to take the shirt from him as he starts looking for pants.

"There was a piano when we were kids. It's sad," he says, "but inevitable, I guess. When you make your living playing music, no matter how much you love it, at some point it becomes a job. You can't be around it all the time. You need some distance." He pulls out a pair of gray flannel pants. "How about these?"

"Sure." I take them from him and just stand there holding the shirt and pants.

"Maybe a sweater, too," Karl says and looks around before noticing the bureau. He walks over to it and pulls open a drawer. "I know I'm that way about law," he says. "I wouldn't do it if I didn't love it, but I have to get away from it, too. Here . . . this one . . ."

He hands me a dark blue V-necked sweater and then laughs. "Okay, you're all set," he says. "Put 'em on and let's have a look."

I'm shy changing clothes in front of Karl. Maybe it's because he'll be looking me over, making an assessment of my appearance. I stand there for a moment, holding the shirt and pants and sweater, not sure how to begin. Karl laughs, not a cruel laugh like Sara's, but a sweet laugh. He points to the bed.

"Put the clothes down," he says. "Or do you want me to hold them?"

"Sure . . . yes," I say, but don't move and Karl has to come over and take the clothes from me.

"The shirt first, okay?"

I start slowly, unbuttoning, discarding, and reach out for the shirt Karl hands me. For a moment I'm bare-chested, then without pants. Karl is oblivious and while this seems normal, it embarrasses me. I want a reaction from him—something besides what he's giving me—but I don't know what sort of reaction would satisfy me. When I'm finished and stand before him in the gray flannel pants, white shirt, and dark blue sweater, he smiles, but I see in his smile a blandness, a perfunctory good-natured niceness that saddens me. He's like a skillful copy of a human being whose beautiful, infuriating smile promises everything but means nothing.

"That's better," Karl says. "Why don't you comb your hair and we'll be all set for Dad's grand entrance."

I nod and a sinking hopelessness comes over me. I'm still calm, though. The pills let me view my hopelessness from a distance then discard it. Whatever I want from Karl, whatever I need from him is buried so deep beneath a slick, reflecting surface that I'll never find it. It's too late now anyway. I go to the mirror above the bureau, pick up the comb, and slowly, deliberately, pull it through my hair. The part forms where it should, exposing my luminous scalp.

"There we go," Karl says, placing his hand on my shoulder. "We're ready."

He doesn't have to lead me downstairs. I leave the room before he does, almost forget he's behind me, until we reach the living room and he moves past me, calling to Mother.

"Mission accomplished," he says with irritating brightness. Mother takes off her apron, wipes her hands, and says, "Let's have a look."

She enters the living room and I notice for the first time that she's wearing a trim blue dress, black pumps, carefully applied makeup, and a cameo on a silver chain around her neck. I didn't understand before, but it's clear now—Dad's homecoming is an event requiring orchestration, timing, and costume changes. Mother's hair is swept up and pinned behind.

She smiles at me and, despite myself, I'm pleased. "That's better," she says, but it's as if I'm not in the room. Her glance darts away from me and back to Karl. "We're finished in the kitchen for a while. Everything's ready to go. I can rest until your father and Sara get home." She sits on one of the overstuffed chairs and through the makeup she looks tired and a bit worried.

"Anything I can do?" Karl asks.

"Nothing, darling." She turns toward me. "Don't you look handsome?" she exclaims, then nods to the sofa. "Why don't you sit down, Michael? We can all have a nice visit before I go back to wife-and-mother mode."

Amy comes out of the kitchen and Karl takes my arm, steering me to the sofa. All three of us sit down across from Mother. Karl's hand rests on Amy's knee.

"Any new ideas for paintings?" Amy asks Mother.

"Some, but I'm taking a break so I can spend more time with Michael. I have no burning desire to paint right now."

"Then what do you do all day?" Karl reaches over and adjusts my shirt collar. His fingers graze the back of my neck and leave a faint tingling behind. "I can't imagine you just sitting around."

"I keep busy."

"She cleans and dusts my room," I say, and Mother seems surprised to hear my voice.

The front door slams open. From where I'm sitting, I don't see anything until Sara stomps into the room, pulling off her hat and scarf, unbuttoning her coat. Mother stands up. Karl bounds past Sara and shouts a greeting. I watch Mother, aware of another shape in my peripheral vision and a scratchy tenor voice crying out in reply. Mother looks happy but mostly just relieved. The shape that is Karl and the shape that must be my dad become one, and I hear the sounds of two men embracing—hands clapping backs in staccato thumps. I turn to see a tall man facing me, looking over the shoulder of his son. He resembles the man on the cover of the compact disc but is older, with more gray hair and a puffiness under his eyes.

"Michael," he says. I expect his voice to match his serious, handsome face, but it's brighter, with an edge of permanent hoarseness. He and Karl disengage and he moves toward me. I have the sensation of wincing, but I stand still and throw my arms around him more from the force of his approach than from affection.

"You look great," Dad says as we hug. Then he pushes me away and holds me at arm's length. I can't look right at him for he has the same blue eyes that Karl has. I know I'm blushing. I look at the wall behind Dad, at the floor, at Mother.

"How are you feeling?" he asks. His smile is both engaging and a bit pathetic, as though he is trying too hard.

"Fine," I say as his grip loosens and he steps away. "Mother's been seeing to things."

"Something she's very good at," Dad says and embraces Mother, then sees Amy and repeats his bear hug on her. "How's my beautiful daughter-in-law?" Everyone seems happy to see him. Even Sara is smiling.

Once the greetings are complete, Dad hangs up his coat in the hall closet, groans about how exhausted he is, moves into the living room, and lowers himself elegantly into one of the overstuffed chairs. As if on cue, the rest of the family begins a series of actions designed to ensure Dad can rest. Karl and Amy go outside to retrieve Dad's luggage, Mother returns to the kitchen, and Sara sits down near Dad in the living room to keep him company. I watch everyone scatter and am left standing just inside the living room. Sara looks at me and although I detect no anger or warning in her gaze, I don't see any sign of welcome either. I move toward the dining room to join Mother in the kitchen when Dad calls to me.

"Come sit by me, Mikey," he says. I hesitate but then move toward him. Sara's gaze follows me.

"I'm so glad you're home again," Dad says, "and that you're recovering. You gave us all quite a scare."

It seems clear that I'm not required to respond and I really don't have anything to say. I try on several expressions—apologetic, concerned, attentive, resigned—then settle into the numb and blank look of one being lectured.

"Your mother tells me you don't remember much about what happened," Dad says, and I nod. "That's probably for the best. I wish I could forget about it as well, but someone always wants to bring up the subject. You'd think I was a celebrity and that what happened is grist for the scandal mill." His face seems to sag a bit as he speaks. He's older now than he was just moments ago. I can't follow everything he's saying, though I understand the words.

"You are a celebrity," Sara says.

"Sweetheart, you're the celebrity in the family." Dad touches Sara's knee. "The other day I had to show my driver's license to cash a check and the cashier asked me if I was related to 'that woman columnist who's so funny.'" He arches his eyebrows and leans toward her. "I assumed she meant you, so I confessed to being your father."

Sara smiles and shakes her head a little. It's attractive, yet when she sees me looking at her, the smile fades again.

Karl and Amy stumble into the entryway loaded with suitcases. They're giggling, and they set the luggage down before coming into the living room.

"I think we got it all," Karl says. His face is flushed from the cold and exertion and his arm encircles Amy's waist, pulling her close. My throat tightens. I'm overwhelmed by the thought that this perfect tableau is wildly wrong, but I have to dismiss it as simple disorientation brought on by a bombardment of family. Too many people I'm supposed to know. Too many memories I'm supposed to have. The air in the living room is getting close. I can hear myself taking deeper breaths, as though fighting for the small amount of oxygen left.

"Let's get these upstairs," Karl says, and he and Amy try to gather up the suitcases again. They giggle. I can hear a suitcase drop to the floor, followed by more giggling.

"Thank God there's nothing breakable in those," Dad says. His words could be jovial, but there is irritation in his tone. "Go help them, Sara," he says. She looks at him, then at me, and hesitates.

Go on, I think and push it out to her. She stands and the look on her face tells me she's doing only what she's told.

"Go on," Dad says. "Mike and I can entertain ourselves for a bit."

She leaves, entering the giggling and bumping but not participating in it. I see Karl and Amy and Sara mount the stairs, suitcases in hand and slung over shoulders. Dad looks at me but says nothing.

"When's dinner?" he shouts toward the dining room, turning slightly, but not taking his eyes off me.

"In about ten minutes," Mother replies.

Dad keeps looking at me, searching for something to say, but just like me he's at a loss. As the silence stretches, I try to think of a way to start a conversation—the weather, his journey home, where he's been, what I did today—but I can't settle on anything, can't be sure I'll make sense to this man who everyone tells me is my father. He's a face on a package come to life. It's as if a character in one of the television programs has suddenly appeared in the living room. He's an anticipation that's materialized before me without hints or directions. I don't know what to do with him now that he's here, nor do I have the confidence that I can fool him as easily as I've fooled Mother. Sweat gathers on my brow. I don't know how long this silence lasts and the more I think about it, the more confused I become. The sweat on my brow slides down my face, following the curve of my cheek. Dad's aging again, his eyes sinking further into their sockets. I can hear the clock ticking now, hear time passing. Dad's mouth opens, his lips form a word and the sound reaches me in a thick, slow blur.

"Mike," he says.

I hear a chime and jump out of my chair. I'm standing at the front door before I even realize that it was the doorbell I heard or that I said, "I'll get it," in the same startled way one says "No!" before being struck on the face. My hand is on the doorknob and in the moment before I turn it, I remember a room flooded with strange yellow light. I hear the sound of a piano and I remember someone sitting close to me, touching my neck.

Standing outside is a tall young man with long blond hair pulled back into a ponytail. His eyes seem to come alive when he sees me. His eyes are pale blue and they look at me, those blue eyes, and although I know I've never seen this man before, I hold my arms out to him.

Paul calls my name.

4

"What are you going to do today?" Paul asks. He stops playing the piano and turns to look at me. I prefer his profile, the line from his forehead to the tip of his prominent nose. I look at other men's profiles when I'm in public now and I see more extreme dips between the brow and the nose, but Paul is beautiful to me for this uniqueness. When I see his full face, I still experience a little shock—it's somewhat asymmetrical, his brow so narrow, his eyes close. As he plays, I study his profile and try to fall in love.

We're in Paul's apartment—"our" apartment, he corrects me—and it hasn't stopped raining for three days. Rain is better than snow for getting around town, but I'm beginning to have a physical reaction to the gray, undifferentiated sky and the sound of pattering on the windows. I sleep all afternoon but am still tired at night. It isn't the pills. I don't have the pills anymore.

It's been three days as well since Paul came for me and brought me here to live. I wanted to, and though the adjustment was a little difficult at first I'm amazed at how quickly I become used to things, to people, to time passing. Paul is very kind, very patient with me, as though he were asking me to forgive him. When he tells me something I've forgotten—where the coffee cups are kept, which key unlocks which door, where I should put my dirty socks—he speaks in a quiet, gentle voice. He tells me he's a teacher and I suppose that prepares him for living with me. In a lot of ways I'm like a child, though I try not to be. It can't be easy, yet Paul doesn't seem to mind. He teaches piano, is a graduate student studying piano, has a piano in the living room of his apartment. Our apartment. Apparently, I was a student, too, and worked as well. I worked in a law firm. I don't remember that and I don't remember Paul—only his voice—but I haven't told him that yet. There's no good time to bring this up, no way to say it that doesn't sound cold. I want my tone to be like Paul's, full of warmth and concern and—I have to assume—love, yet when I speak I hear an empty sound that no change of volume or speed or inflection can hide. It's like the background hiss on a recording, easy to ignore unless you're listening for it. When you're aware, though, it pervades everywhere and ruins everything.

"What are you going to do today?" Paul asks. I know he has to go out for most of the day to give private piano lessons. This is how he pays the rent on our apartment, he tells me. A little more money comes from the university, not much, and Paul says it's enough for us to get by. I don't eat much. There are no more prescriptions, no more visits to doctors now. When Paul's not here, I sleep a lot or I look out the window and watch people and cars go by on the street. Perhaps some day I can help out, get a job. I don't need much.

"Maybe I'll read a book," I say. Paul doesn't own a television. "I'll listen to some music." I can't concentrate enough to read, so sometimes I just sit on the sofa with a book open in front of me. It's comforting. Sometimes I turn the pages and, when I get up, I place a strip of cardboard in the book to save my place, as though I were really reading after all.

"Try some Mozart," Paul says and gets up from the piano bench to flip through some compact discs and pick out my selections for the day. I've been listening to what he suggests. The music is soothing, like Paul's voice. Often the music makes me drowsy, though it could be the rain that does this. I dream of vivid colors and sounds, of strange cosmic landscapes, and of Sasha. The images are disjointed, and I remember none of the specifics. I hear music, too, but I know it isn't the Handel or Haydn that Paul has chosen. It's lush, this dream music, overheated, shifting, and sometimes dissonant. It rushes over me like a wave and I wake up sweating. Other than Sasha, I remember no people in the dreams—not Paul, not my family—but for a second or two after waking, I expect to see Mother come into the room. It's the only time I think of her and the old life from which Paul has taken me.

I hear Mother say, "Who is it?" from somewhere inside the house. Paul and I are standing just outside the front door. He's holding me, hugging me so tight I can barely breathe. It's wonderful, though, and I put my arms around him, smell his skin, his hair, press against him with a force I don't really understand. He is taller than I am. I turn my head and lay my cheek on his breast, which is not soft but warm and solid and comforting. He kisses the top of my head and murmurs words I can't hear.

Behind me, Mother says, "Oh," as if someone has knocked the wind out of her. I know she's standing there, but for a moment longer nothing can make me leave Paul's arms. He isn't the man I pictured from his voice. In fact, he's physically the opposite of what I remember and, rather than frightening me, the relief of his presence, the reality of him, holds me to this spot like a heavy, calming weight.

Paul looks at Mother over the top of my head and says, in a low voice, "Hello, Marta."

She doesn't speak at first. I imagine her expression has the same bewilderment and affront I hear in her voice. "I told you this wasn't a good time," she says.

"Yes," Paul replies. "I know what you said, but you hung up before I told you I was coming anyway."

Paul releases his grip. I turn around to see Mother staring at me and Dad stern, his hands on her shoulder as if to steady her or keep her from floating away. He isn't looking at me or even at Paul but focuses at some point in the front yard.

"It's freezing," Dad says. "Come in and close the door."

"We were just about to sit down to dinner," Mother says.

"I've already eaten," Paul replies.

Dad moves forward, pulls me and Paul into the house, and says, low and quick, "Can we please close the door," as he slams it shut. I can hear Dad breathing. Mother doesn't move. Paul shakes Dad's hand off his arm and steps away, letting me go and brushing his shirtsleeve as though he's been soiled.

Sara comes down the stairs, followed by Karl and Amy. "Who are you?" Sara asks. We must make a strange sight, the four of us. She sounds surprised.

"You must be Sara," Paul says.

"Paul!" Karl shouts, taking the remaining steps two at a time. His boisterousness is so out of place that I sense a palpable shift in the air, as though the molecules begin vibrating faster.

Karl shakes Paul's hand. "Mom didn't say you were coming," he says.

"I think we should all sit down," Dad says and gestures to the living room with a nod. His breathing is quiet now. I can barely hear it.

Paul is pale. The skin on his neck is supple, but with a hardness like stone. His Adam's apple fascinates me. I watch him swallow, see the muscles of this neck move.

"Hello, Karl," Paul says, "Amy."

Amy glances from Karl to Paul, then at Mother and Dad. She's taking the situation in and although she's smiling, there is a tentativeness about her. She nods to Paul. "What a nice surprise," she says and seems to mean it, though another look at Mother stops her smile.

Dad gestures again. Karl takes Paul's coat and everyone moves into the living room warily, like cats slinking past one another. I'm the last one to leave the hallway. No one seems to notice. If I went upstairs and locked myself in my room, I wonder how long it would take them to realize I was gone. I could even make a run for it. The front door is closed but so near to me. A few quiet steps, a gentle tug, a little whoosh of air, and I'd be gone. But it's cold and I don't know where my coat is. The sun is setting.

"Michael," Dad calls from the living room.

Mother is gone, but I can hear her in the kitchen and dining room, moving about and setting down plates and silverware with a great deal of clatter. Everyone else but Sara is sitting down and looking at the carpet, the walls, and occasionally at one another. Sara leans against the wall near the dining room, scowling. When I come into the room and stand, looking for someplace to go, she sighs and goes to help Mother set the table. Paul is on the sofa and motions for me to join him. As I do, Dad's expression fills me with satisfaction. There's the slightest furrow in his brow and a priggish purse to his lips.

"I've come to see how Mike is doing," Paul says.

"He's doing well," Dad says. "Improving."

"I'd like to hear that from Mike," Paul says to Dad but turns to me.

It's easier to look at Paul when he's concentrating on someone or something else. I want my eyes to meet his, but I'm too nervous. Instead I look at his thin pink lips, at some renegade hairs that have eluded his ponytail, at the striking marble smoothness of his cheeks. He doesn't seem real. If I touch his face, my fingers will glide along a cool, strong surface.

"I'm . . . I sleep a lot," I say and am silent for what seems like a long time. I can hear Dad shifting in his chair. Karl coughs. A clock somewhere ticks off the seconds. I try to concentrate on things, on facts. Feelings are suspect right now. Feelings can't tell me how I'm doing. Only facts can do that. "Sometimes I run in place . . ." My voice trails off. I look around and see these people staring at me, waiting. I open my mouth, but everything I can think of saying halts before it comes up my throat. I close my mouth again. All I can do is signal to them. All I can do is shrug and look away.

"Mike," Paul says, very softly. His hand is on my shoulder. The clock won't stop ticking, and it seems to grow louder until Mother calls from the dining room.

"Dinner," she shouts, then leans into the room and says again, "Dinner," with a clipped, singsong chirping. Nobody moves. "It's time for dinner," she says and turns away.

"Mike," Paul says. I've been drifting again. He's no longer sitting at the piano, but comes into the living room wearing his coat and carrying some spiral-bound scores. "I won't be late," he says. "You sure you'll be OK?"

"I'll be fine."

"There's sandwich meat in the fridge for lunch."

"Sure," I say. "Really, I'll be fine."

Paul hugs me and gives me a quick kiss.

"I know you will," he says. "You're doing really well." He holds me for a moment, looking into my eyes as if he were searching for something. I force myself to look back and not turn away. It's getting easier to do this. It's quite pleasurable, actually. I think about making Paul late, doing things to him like we did the first night I came here.

"You're not sorry you're here with me, are you?" Paul asks and my previous thought embarrasses me.

"No," I say and can feel myself blushing. "No, I want to be here." Paul smiles, then kisses me again.

"I have to go," he says.

For a long while after the door closes, the apartment is quiet and I continue to stand in the living room, just looking at the wall. Paul's kiss lingers on my skin like a drop of hot wax, cooling.

"Look, I really didn't come here to eat," Paul says to Mother. "I'd like to talk to Mike for a moment in private."

Mother presses her lips together, then speaks in a polite, controlled voice. "We're about to sit down and eat, Paul. I'm sure this can wait."

"Yes," Dad says. "We'll all feel better after a good meal."

"No, really . . ." Paul touches my arm again. "Mike, I need to talk to you in private."

Everyone is looking at me, waiting for me to make a decision, to say something. Or so it seems. I can't imagine any of them doing as I say.

"Maybe . . . upstairs . . . my room," I say. "Just for a minute." I want it to sound decisive, but it comes out like a question, as though I'm asking for permission. Mother just turns to go back into the kitchen, and as she goes she says, "Talk, talk, go ahead and talk."

Even though I make the suggestion, it's Paul who acts upon it. He stands up and waits for me to join him. Dad doesn't speak or even look at us. Karl and Amy just smile, though Karl nods slightly, indicating it's OK for me to go with Paul. Our eyes meet as he nods, and I think, *You could stop me if you wanted to,* with some disappointment, so I get up, walk across the living room, into the hallway, and up the stairs. I don't need to turn around. I know Paul is there.

In my room, Paul closes the door, comes from behind, and pulls me close. I feel his lips on the back of my neck, then he spins me around. I'm looking into his eyes and everything seems to stop except the blood rushing in my ears. I know what's coming, know it's all happening very fast even if nothing seems to move, and I stretch my body upward as Paul leans down. When our lips meet, a warm shock passes through me, pushing me into him. It's the first kiss I remember. This hunger is new to me, this thirst as his tongue slides over mine. There's an instinct to my actions. I suck, trying to draw him into me, but before I'm satisfied, he pulls his tongue back, though our lips don't stop. We repeat this, alternating tongues, pushing, pulling, breaking apart, coming together, until I have to rest my head against his chest and catch my breath. I hear his thundering heart. Neither of us speaks.

"Mike," Paul says at last in a whisper. He doesn't expect a response but keeps saying my name as if he's reciting an incantation. An ache pushes up inside me, trying to form words but coming too fast, past my throat, past my mouth, and pouring out as tears. I have to breathe, but all I can do is sob and gasp for air. If I could speak, I would tell Paul everything, tell him only the truth—what I know, what I don't remember, how I feel, how his kiss has changed me—but I can only imagine the words and hold him closer.

"Everything's fine now, Mike," he says, stroking my hair. "I'm here. Everything's fine."

I want this sensation to stay until I know what it is, until I can give it a name.

"How fast can you pack?" Paul asks. "You don't have much here, do you?"

I realize what Paul wants and know I should leave. I understood this before, yet it surprises me, and when the words do come out, they are a stutter of disconnected phrases.

"I can help you, Mike." He breaks away from me and moves to the closet. "Where's your suitcase?"

The space where his body was still seems to press against me. I have no idea where my suitcase is or what I have here that I would want to take with me.

"I don't know," I say. "I . . . I don't remember."

I've spoken the truth and the weight against my chest is gone. I turn to see if Paul notices, if he realizes the significance of my words, but he can't. Nobody can.

"Of course you remember," he says with a little laugh as he opens the closet. "It's right here." He pulls it out and takes it over to the bed where he opens it and then looks at me. "Come on," he says.

I still can't move, can't make my eyes meet his.

"Mike," he says as though I haven't heard him, then says again, "Mike" and there's a fear in his voice that tears at me. I turn to him.

"You want to come with me, don't you?" He says it as if this is the first time any doubt occurs to him. When I don't answer him immediately, the muscles in his face relax and his expression triggers my tears again.

"What?" Paul says. He's tired, exasperated. I can hear it. "Mike. What? Do you want to come with me or not?" Instantly, though, his tone changes and he's holding me again, telling me to hush, telling me he's here to look after me.

"I'll pack for you," he whispers. "Whatever we forget, we can buy at home."

That word again. Yet when Paul says it, it sounds comforting or at least less confusing. I almost believe we have a home, can almost picture what it must look like—this life we're supposed to have. I wipe my nose, run my hand across my face, and sniffle.

"The stuff in the bureau," I say. "I don't think there's much else."

It's the first time I see him smile like this—a smile of joy and relief—as he pulls the bureau drawers open and throws T-shirts and underwear to me. I'm delirious with freedom, laughing as I pile the clothes in the suitcase, not even bothering to fold them.

"Don't worry about your parents," Paul says when we finish. "They can't stop you from going. You're an adult. You've been released from the hospital. There's nothing they can do. Remember that."

"Yes," I say.

"Anything else?" Paul asks, looking around the room.

"Yes . . . no . . . nothing."

My heart is beating fast, pounding so loudly I can't hear Paul speak. He's asking me something. His lips move and all I can do is look at him and smile until he takes hold of my shoulders and gives me a firm shake.

"Mike," I hear him say. "Did they give you any medication?" He looks right at me but speaks as if I'm far away from him. "Any pills you need to take with?"

I know the answer to this and I say, "No." I don't see what good the pills will do me anymore. Everything is different now. My life—that part I remember—divides itself neatly into past and future at this moment, with this heartbeat, with this blink of my eye.

"I'm fine," I say. Paul can't imagine how truthful I am right now, even as I lie to him. "There aren't any pills." I close the suitcase and stand up. "This is it," I say. "This is everything."

Standing in the middle of Paul's living room, I try to decide what I should do first. The day stretches before me and although there's nothing I have to accomplish, I want an answer to Paul's inevitable question. He'll come home around five and ask, "What did you do today?" The first time, I had nothing to say. I sat and looked out the front window, watching people walk by in the rain. Paul lives on the first floor, but raised above the street quite a bit, and no one looks up as they walk. I could watch people all day long and never be seen. I justified this watching by telling myself that I could remember so few people and maybe that's why I'm disconnected, why I always scramble to understand what people are doing and saying. Of course, the truth was different. Watching required nothing of me. I only had to sit on the arm of the sofa by the window. A steady stream of people—mostly young, mostly students with backpacks—would move past me. At first I tried to make assumptions about individuals based on their walk or clothes or whether they looked in front of them or at the ground as they walked. Before long, though, I'd realize I hadn't noticed anyone for a while.

At the end of the day, Paul had asked me, "What did you do today?" and I had said, "I watched people going by on the street." Paul tried not to show his discomfort. I understand why. I was wasting my day, not being productive. It was, perhaps, a sign that I hadn't improved. Today would be different. Today I would do something, have an answer.

So I stand in the living room and I wonder what to do. Listen to music, maybe. That way Paul and I could talk about what I'd heard. Maybe I could dust the apartment. I can hear our upstairs neighbor stomping back and forth above me. It annoys Paul, the amount of noise this man makes, and I have to admit I don't understand why he runs across his living room so much, back and forth, so loud you'd think he wore enormous boots or that he was a big man. Paul's spoken to him. He's a small man, Paul says, who claims he always goes shoeless in his apartment. "He's just naturally loud," Paul adds with sarcasm.

I think about what would make Paul happy, what I can do that will make it look as if I've improved. It does no good to think about what would make me happy. I lack objectivity. I can't measure anything because the reference points just aren't there. Listening to music seems the best choice. I'll have something to say.

The disc is already in the player—Paul must have put it there—so all I have to do is press a button. When the music begins, it rolls across the room in a loud wave. The man upstairs stomps. I lunge for the volume control and the music recedes, tinkling like crystal. I adjust the level until the sound is smooth, until it glides into my head and I relax, sitting right there on the floor, folding my legs under me.

This is Mozart.

For a moment, I pay attention to the music, following the thread of a melody until it melts into the harmony and then I'm not sure where one thread starts and the other ends, just aware of a change. The disc's plastic container says *Jupiter Symphony*. I listen for sounds of planets but hear none. I hear mountains and forests in the effortless workings of the strings and the triumph of the brass.

Paul is driving. The sun has set and the headlights illuminate gray snow piles on both sides of a road that's black like glistening rubber. Paul hums softly, hums along with the barely audible radio. He thinks I'm asleep and, though he's near, his humming seems to come from a great distance. I'm leaning against the passenger-side door, my head turned toward him, my eyes barely closed.

I don't remember any dramatics when we left the house, no one blocking our way or threatening to call the police. Paul kept his hand on my shoulder or on my arm and I knew that if he broke that contact I would change my mind, fall down in a heap and let Dad and Karl drag me back up to my room. There was a pulse, a current flowing between Paul and me. It pricked my skin, entered me, moving up my arm, spinning around in my chest, vibrating my heart and ribs.

I don't recall saying anything, though I must have confirmed that I was choosing to leave. I must have spoken sincerely, convincingly. Before we turned to go, I caught a glimpse of Mother and Dad. They stood next to each other, Dad's hand on Mother's shoulder, and I imagined they were a reflection of Paul and myself and of Amy and Karl, too, like we were all standing in a room of mirrors. Dad's face was silent, perhaps contemptuous, perhaps a little bored. Mother's lips were pinched shut, making her look angry, but her eyes were wide and desperate. Then she glanced at the floor, turned away, and left the room. Dad's hand dropped to his side. We were gone.

As we drove into the night, I thought about sex. I contemplated the heat and the thrill when Paul touched me. I stole glances at him as he drove, watching his Adam's apple move as he swallowed, admired the line of his profile and the way his hair was pulled back so tightly into a ponytail. He leaned forward to adjust the heat and I saw a muscle in his arm flex. My penis stiffened and burned against my thigh. I pressed my legs together slowly as if I'd shifted in my sleep and a radiant pleasure moved up my body, making me gasp. I fell asleep several times and dreamed of our bodies touching, dreamed of a kiss that went on and on.

I'm not sure how long the drive took. Hours and hours. It was still dark when we parked in front of a tall, narrow house on a tree-lined street. Paul was exhausted, barely said a word as we got out of the car and walked up the weathered front steps. He carried my suitcase.

Paul lived on the first floor of the house and now, it seemed, so did I. The hallway was not even three feet wide and had a single lightbulb near the door, which made the apartment beyond seem shadowy and vague. Paul placed his arm around my shoulder.

"Welcome home," he said and gently pushed me into the living room, where he set down my suitcase and fumbled for the light switch. I hoped that the light would reveal a familiar place. I wanted a flash of recognition, my memory rolling over me with a cold, bright finality. When the lamp came on, I blinked and then opened my eyes to a room about half the size of Mother and Dad's living room. An upright piano was against one wall and a mad scatter of music scores covered the floor. Against the other wall was a large plaid sofa, some stereo equipment, and several shelves full of compact discs. There was dust in the air and a dusty smell. I couldn't remember having seen any of this before. My sense of failure became physical and my stomach ached as if I was hungry.

Paul hugged me and kissed the top of my head. I knew he was exhausted. He pushed me toward one of the two doors leading from the living room. The light penetrated far enough to see the shadowy bulk of a bed and a tangle of sheets. I hesitated.

"I'm so tired," Paul said and I yielded.

In bed he held me, but it was without heat. We fell asleep within seconds of lying down.

The music comes to an end. Another movement begins, a slower tempo, different from the previous but soon indistinguishable from it. Sitting here, listening, I don't really see the difference between this and watching people passing on the street. In both cases, I'm quiet and still. In both cases, my mind won't stay long on one thought.

My first morning in our apartment, I woke up from a dream of sex to find Paul pressed close against my back. His penis was stiff and hot along the curve of my ass. I wasn't sure if he was awake or asleep at first, but then he moved his hips and thrust against me. I responded, moving closer, though there was no space between us, and he reached around to stroke my erection. It all happened quite effortlessly, as if we had done this many times before. I didn't think about where my hands went or what my mouth should do.

I'm struck by the spaces between what I remember. These spaces are different from my memory lapses, which are maddening for their absences and their tantalizing promise that if I try harder, if I just concentrate and focus, every detail will return in a simultaneous flash. I can remember specific moments of that morning in bed—the first taste of Paul's tongue, ripe and pungent and so pleasurable; the silky feel of his skin as I ran my hand along his ribs; the shock of hunger as I took Paul's penis in my mouth. I opened my eyes as I sucked and saw him looking down at me, his lips parted in a gasp and a smile—these images are all so clear, but their continuity is forgotten. What happened in between is missing. It's vague, so unimportant.

Paul climaxed first and the tensing of his muscles triggered something in me, as though a switch was thrown. My excitement intensified, washed over me, and after I ejaculated my body grew numb. There was a singing in my head. I wondered if this was what fainting was like. I knew Paul was near, that his body was close to me, but he seemed so far away.

The telephone rings. I turn down the stereo's volume and hesitate a moment before getting up and taking the receiver.

"Hello," I say and expect it to be Paul. *Just wanted to see how you're doing,* he'd say. *See if everything's all right.*

"Michael," Mother says.

"Yes," I say after a long pause. "Hello, Mother."

"I'm just calling to see how you are."

"I'm fine, Mother. Really."

"You forgot your pills."

"Paul got me another prescription," I say. It's a lie. I have no drugs now and no trouble staying quiet on my own.

"I talked to Dr. Jamison. He's concerned. He doesn't think you're ready to be away from home, and I agree."

"I am home, Mother. This is where I lived before . . ."

"And you remember that?" she asks. She tries to hide her sarcasm, but she can't, not entirely.

"Yes," I say with conviction. "Yes, I do." Another lie, but things seem comfortable here—smaller, easier to understand.

"I don't believe you."

I sigh into the receiver.

"I think Paul has an enormous amount of influence over you and not necessarily for the better," she says. "I don't think you're capable of making your own decisions. Not yet. I saw how you are. We all did."

"You're entitled to your opinion," I say, as though I'm reading lines off a piece of paper. "All of you. But I'm an adult. I can make up my own mind."

She sighs. "Is he there now?"

"In the shower."

"So late? What about work?"

"Teacher's hours."

We don't speak for several seconds. "Anything else?" I ask.

Quietly, she says, "You can always come back. If things don't work out, you're always welcome here."

"Hang on," I say and cover the receiver with my palm, pretending Paul is calling me. I wait a beat, then tell Mother, "I have to go."

"All right. I love you."

It's the first time I remember her saying that to me. It sounds appended and a bit unnatural.

"Yes," I say. "Good-bye."

The music is still softly playing, but I've no desire to turn the volume up. Listening strikes me as too passive, so I get up and walk over to the piano, wondering if I ever knew how to play. As I sit down on the bench, I wait for my hands and fingers to remember. I place them over the keys and wait. Nothing comes. I bring my fingers closer and lightly touch some of the white keys. Still nothing. No one has told me I played the piano, but it seems odd if I didn't. A spiral-bound score is open on the piano's music rest. I study it for a moment. Some things about it I understand. I know that each note represents a finger on a key. When the notes are on top of each other, that means the keys are struck at the same time. The shapes of the notes have to do with how long they are held.

What are the pedals for? How do I know which note corresponds to which key? It would only take knowing one to unlock the mystery. The rest would fall in place and I could decipher the music like some coded message. The closer I study the score, though, the less sure I am of a solution. There are other marks—hash marks, little Bs, dots, and elegant curls. Hesitant, I strike one key, the white key closest to the middle, then move up the keyboard, striking one white key after another and listening to the sounds ascend in an orderly expected way. When I reach the end, I start again at the lowest white key and this time move up the alternating black keys and white keys in sequence, receiving little shocks of pleasure from the unexpected sounds. I come to the end and again I start over, faster this time, pecking the white keys with one hand and the black keys with the other. This takes more coordination, but I make it all the way to the end without missing a note, giggling in triumph.

One more time I start at the lowest key and try to move faster, but somewhere around the middle of the keyboard I stop, remembering an image that takes me away from the piano, the living room, the apartment. I see a corridor and on the floor are alternate black and white stripes like the keys of a piano. If I step forward, a note will sound. If I run down the corridor, I'll produce a sweep of notes just as I did at the piano. At the other end of the hall is a room full of equipment. I recall a buzzing sound, salve on my temples, a white light.

I shake my head. I'm back in the living room, an icy sweat on my brow. *I've done something wrong,* I think. *But what?*

The clock says eleven. I'm tired, but I don't want to sleep. It's too early for a nap, but my thoughts turn to the bedroom and I get up from the piano bench, walk to the doorway, look at the unmade bed. The sheets are white, but in the darkened room they look gray and plastic, as though molded into permanent disarray. I touch them to be sure they'll move and a scent rises from the disturbed sheets—the smell of bodies and hair and sweat, sensual and narcotic. It draws me close. I fall into the sheets face down, each hand grabbing a bunch of cloth and crumpling it as I breathe in the messy, human aroma of my life. I turn over, facing the ceiling, and try to remember this room, make it seem familiar, see the place in a flash of recognition. To one side of the bed is a wall of closet doors, not unlike my room at Mother and Dad's house, but without the mirrors. There is no desk or chest of drawers—the room is too small—just a nightstand and a window that opens onto a light well, letting in only a murky illumination. One of the closet doors is open, revealing a dark tangle of cloth and wire hangers. The closet is full of clothes—my clothes and Paul's clothes, crammed together with no attempt at order. Piles of boxes cover the closet floor and are stacked on a shelf that runs above the clothes rack. The knobs on the doors are round and gold. I get up from the bed and take a step toward the closet. I've thought about those boxes several times in the past three days, wondering if they contain parts of my life. The apartment itself is uncluttered, even though it's so small. Aside from a framed photo of Paul and me—our shoulders bare, our heads cocked toward each other and touching as we face the camera with silly grins—I don't see many items that tell me much. The titles of the books and compact discs and magazines— they mean nothing to me. The boxes in the closet are promising. A place to keep personal things, out of sight. Despite this, I have avoided them, not exactly afraid of what I'd find, but not eager to explore the contents either.

Today, I have no more excuses. I take two steps toward the open closet. Cars pass by outside. The clocks tick. Mozart plays softly and sounds far, far away.

I reach the closet and put out my hand in front of me, running my fingers along the boxes on the shelf. None of them is labeled. They are large and appear heavy. The shelf sags slightly. On the floor are smaller boxes, sometimes stacked two or three high. Half of them are shoeboxes, and several others are boxes for papers or books. I sit on the floor and carefully push the other closet door open.

The first box contains scores and sheet music, the pages covered with markings and lines like some ancient language I can't decipher. They're beautiful but cannot speak to me. Mixed in with the printed scores are notebooks filled with handwritten musical notation, elegant and symmetrical. Paul's name is written on the covers. I flip through the pages slowly, marveling at his steady hand and the mysterious markings. Some people can look at this and hear music. How?

I replace the cover of that box, make sure I return the box to its original position, then open several others in succession. Old tennis shoes, paperback books, some official looking government forms covered with numbers. Then I decide to open a box at the bottom of a stack of three, which is in the farthest corner from me behind a pair of dusty black boots. I remove the boxes on top of it, checking their contents. I move quietly and slowly, as though I am an intruder and someone is sleeping on the living-room sofa. More shoes, more music scores. The first thing I find in the bottom box is a stack of typewritten pages. The top piece of paper is a letter on the stationary of a literary agent.

Dear Mr. Van Allen:

Thank you for submitting sample chapters from your novel, *Future Imperfect*. Sara hadn't mentioned you would be sending them or told me she had a brother who is a writer, so I apologize for the amount of time it took me to reply.

I'm sorry to tell you that I am not interested in representing the book. Parts of it are well written, but it lacks narrative drive and at times is difficult going. If I'm not compelled to read it, how can I expect others to do so? In addition, it's somewhat derivative of Thomas Pynchon and Gabriel García Márquez, though without the wild imagination of those writers. Even in the space of these fifty pages, the fantastic elements seem forced and I get the impression I'm supposed to be dazzled when, in fact, I'm mostly just confused.

That said, there is some good stuff here. Best of luck with your attempts to place the book, though I suspect you'd have better luck writing another, more straightforward novel.

Sincerely,
J. C. Cavanaugh

There are five other letters, all from literary agencies, all much shorter than the first one, all rejecting the book. Beneath the letters, I find another box. I can tell when I lift it that it contains a manuscript. I remove the cover and see the title page:

Future Imperfect
or
Armageddon and I've Nothing to Wear

A novel in three parts and a coda
by
Michael Van Allen

I flip through the pages that follow, keeping them in the box. All the pages are covered with typewritten words. The last page is numbered 576. I've written a book.

It seems absurd, as though the book has materialized out of nothing. I can't imagine coming up with that many words and covering that many pages. There is no typewriter in the apartment. How did I type it?

I've written a book.

I remove the title page, placing it on the floor.

Part I

Prologue
On the afternoon of that day, on the day of that month in the year when it happened, Antonius Septimus Jeremiah Junior (whom everyone called Andy) dozed by the phosphorescent green drainage ditch running through his backyard and dreamed he had grown antennae that were two feet long and lovely blue wings.

On the same afternoon of that day in the month of the year when it happened, in a house by another drainage ditch (though this one glowed pink) in another city far away, Priscilla Pennywort dreamed a remarkably similar dream. Her wings were yellow and her eyes became prisms. She woke up when the sky flashed.

There was a boom.

Everyone looked up on the afternoon of the day in the month of the year that it happened.

It was happening.

The words make little sense. I remove more pages and scan for anything understandable. I flip through pages and soon realize it's mostly gibberish. So I replace the title page and the box cover, lifting the manuscript and its box out of the larger box, and arrange the rejection letters on top. Still inside the box is a stack of photographs, flattened by the weight of the manuscript. I remove them as well. They're not glossy like the photographs at Mother and Dad's house. They're stiff, as though they had dried in the sun. The photographs are black and white and have no people in them. Instead, I recognize parts of objects in close-up—a telephone receiver, a wet spoon, tangled shoelaces, some candy—with deep shadows stretching from them. It's as if the photographer tried to make the objects unrecognizable but didn't quite succeed. Under the photographs are negatives, arranged in a plastic sheet. A label on the sheet has my name and a date five years earlier.

Then, I reach the bottom of the box. There are three folded pieces of paper—programs for plays performed by the university drama department with dates from eight years ago. I open each program and my name jumps out at me even though it's quite small.

I am twenty-nine years old now. At twenty-one, I was an actor. Rosencrantz in *Hamlet,* Ralph Waldo Emerson in *The Night Thoreau Spent in Jail,* Second Roustabout in *Carnival.*

I wait for the lightning strike of memory to hit. I've dug down through layers of my past and unearthed precious artifacts—some broken and enigmatic, some perfectly preserved. I wait. Nothing comes. This is a box containing someone's life. I pack it away, making sure to replace everything just as I found it.

I close both closet doors and back away, then turn around suddenly, struck by the thought that something is under the bed. Dropping to my knees, I look. At first, I'm disappointed. I was wrong. All I see are billows of dust, a broken umbrella, and a piece of wood. The sensation that made me look seemed so much like remembering, yet I have no idea what I expected to find. Then I notice a rip in the cloth covering the bottom of the box spring. It's large enough for my hand to fit, and so, as I'm sure I've done so many times before, I reach inside the bed. A spring prevents me from inserting my hand too far. I move along the cloth bottom and touch the surface of a hard and flat and smooth object. I push it toward the rip. A worn notebook slips out, landing on the floor and sending a cloud of dust into my face.

It has stiff cardboard covers and a sewn spine and *Composition Notebook* printed across the front. Beneath those words someone has written *MVA,* my initials and also Mother's. Carefully, I open the notebook and look at the handwriting that fills the first page. I flip ahead a few pages, then more, and finally look at the last pages. They're blank, but the other pages are filled with words, all written in the same fast, sloping handwriting, all written by me.

part two

yearning

1

He moved like a gazelle. Like a hyena
He moved like a blue jay. Like a sunrise

XxXxXx

At sunrise, the moon, a sliver missing from one side, is set in the deepest blue, a kind of blue that goes from almost white to deepest midnight in an unbroken spectrum, the changes barely perceptible. Then the horizon starts to show a violent band of red, perfectly demarcated from the blue, just the faintest rupture of white at one point—a distant cloud, the trail of a jet? The hills are black against the red. Colors begin to separate upward into the sky. You think you've found the dividing line between the red, the orange, the lightest green, the white, the blue, but each time you look again, that line is gone or moved, become less distinct.

XxXxXx

Cinderella Schubert, or A Tale of Two Franzs

Once upon a time, there was a young man named Patrick Von Nella who was the son of a great man and a great woman. He had everything a young man could want—health, comfort, good looks, prospects—but he was lonely for a companion, for another man. Unlike many of his friends, Patrick didn't have the image of his young man firmly formed in his mind. He knew he wanted someone kind and tall, a companion he could depend on, grow old with. But if someone asked him to elaborate, Patrick sputtered and wondered. A dark man, perhaps. Someone who reads. He could be blond, too. A ticklish man, but not too ticklish. A man with hair where men should have hair.

So Patrick went through life lonely and looking for his companion everywhere. In glittering parks at noon. Along roadsides. Down dark alleys. At school and at home. Everywhere. One night, Patrick heard his friends chattering about a costume ball that was to take place in a week. It would be an enormous party, and Patrick knew that meant many young men would attend. He set about finding the perfect costume. Not flashy, yet noticeable.

Not subdued, but not garish either. He searched and he searched, but on the evening before the ball Patrick still had nothing to wear. He wandered the streets of his town in a daze until he came upon a dusty little costume shop he'd never heard of around a corner he hadn't noticed before.

"What do you have in the way of costumes?" Patrick asked the pale young clerk.

"We're almost cleared out," the clerk said, "on account of the ball. But I do have one costume left. You look about the right size for it."

"What is it?" Patrick asked. "Not too gaudy, I hope."

"It's called Composer," the clerk said. "Sort of a generic nineteenth-century-composer outfit. Waistcoat, starched collar, cravat, rectangular wire glasses, and an optional wig, which you won't need. You've got plenty of hair."

"Just a generic Composer," Patrick pouted. "It seems so drab."

"Try it on," the clerk said. "We'll see which composer you resemble most."

Patrick agreed. When he emerged from the changing room, the clerk messed up Patrick's hair until it looked like a tangled mane, took a step back, and stared at him.

"Franz Schubert," the clerk said.

Patrick looked in the mirror. "Gustav Mahler, maybe."

The clerk shook his head.

"Schubert," he said. "It's uncanny. Do you want the costume or not? You don't have much time left until the ball."

"Yes," Patrick said, "I suppose." When the transaction was complete, Patrick rushed home to get ready for the big night. He decided, as he showered and primped, that the best plan of attack for the ball was simple observation. After he arrived, Patrick hung back, watching the costumed party-goers laughing and talking and drinking. Very soon, he noticed a tall young man with long blond hair swept back and falling to his shoulders. The man was wearing the same generic Composer costume that Patrick wore, though without the wire glasses. At the moment Patrick saw the young man, the young man noticed Patrick and his costume. Both of them smiled and Patrick walked over to him.

"Hello," Patrick said. "You look like Franz Lizst."

"Very good," the young man replied. "I was afraid no one would guess. And you are . . ."

"Franz Schubert," Patrick said.

"Ah." The young man took Patrick's hand. "My name is Raul."

"Patrick."

"You make a very handsome composer, Patrick."

"So do you, Raul."

And they did indeed live happily ever after. Well, for a while. For a long while, actually. They had wonderful Sunday mornings reading *The New York Times* as they lay entwined in each other's arms. They shared kisses that were perfectly in tune. They both had a love of music. Patrick enjoyed watching Raul play the theremin and hearing him weave electric melodies out of the air with the motion of his hands. Patrick and Raul were companions and lovers and friends. And it really didn't matter whether—

Hup two three four Hup two three four

XxXxXx

A Saturday afternoon in November was approaching the time of twilight, and the vast tract of unenclosed wild known as Egdon Heath embrowned itself moment by moment.

XxXxXx

Can't sleep. It was my twenty-ninth birthday today and we went for dinner at Passpourtout where I had some sort of eggplant vinaigrette concoction and Paul worked his way through an inoffensive Caesar Salad and some Chicken Kiev. We toasted to me.

Gifts and cards arrived over the last few days from Mother and Dad (another tasteful vase) and Karl and Aimless (Book—*The Private Lives of Great Composers*). Paul presented his gift in person: a hunter green and blue flannel shirt. No card, no nothing from Sara. She's still so pissed at me for writing to her agent. Obviously getting paid for her pathetic opinions and having millions of people hanging on her every word makes her superior to those of us who really work for a living. Someone should pay me for mouthing banal chitchat. My ideas are just as interesting and, at the least, more colorful than hers. When Paul and I got home, incoming phone calls from Mother and Karl. Sara has vowed never to speak to me again. Dad is too exhausted and probably forgot, but he'll catch me tomorrow or the next day, mock-begging for mock-forgiveness. Paul's been asleep for hours. Tomorrow, I'll ask him about going to Karl and Amy's cabin over Labor Day and of course he'll say yes. He loves Karl and Amy and vice versa. Maybe they should adopt him.

XxXxXx

Idea for a story: A man wakes up one day and realizes he doesn't have a single friend. He sets out to make three new friends within twenty-four hours. Sort of a Ulysses lite. Challenge: how to make this interesting and dramatic without being pathetic.

XxXxXx

Idea for a book: Son of famous baseball player doesn't make Little League, so the boy attempts suicide but later realizes there's no point to doing even that. Sort of an existential young adult book. Challenge: would have to do research on baseball.

XxXxXx

Idea for an article: An examination of the shallowness of contemporary newspaper journalism, targeting smart-ass, trendy columnists. Challenge: how to write about shallowness without being shallow.

XxXxXx

Can't move anything past the idea stage. Would be easier to write about myself or how everything relates to me—like Sara does—but who wants to read about being a file clerk in a law firm when you're almost thirty years old? Who wants to read what it's like to be an average student at a large university and then stay on after graduation like a lingering cold? Idea: write about what it's like growing up in a famous family. Except I never really paid much attention to all that. Dad's fame resided "over there." It never intruded into our day-to-day lives.

Still, there's nothing like riding on Dad and Mother and Sara's coattails. At least I know people would want to read about them.

Douglas Van Allen always knew he would be famous. Some people just do, regardless of talent or luck. Grandfather was self-made. Single-handedly, he amassed a fortune in real estate before he married Grandmother, so Douglas—born into a comfort that allowed for the indulgence of talent and artistic tendencies—grew up knowing that if his music and piano playing went nowhere, he could always have a good job selling real estate. Failure, of course, wasn't to be a worry. Could anyone so gifted doubt his gift? And of course, anyone so gifted might assume his children would inherit similar gifts. After all, they were exposed to music, art, literature, theater from an early age. They were encouraged to participate—art lessons, piano lessons, acting lessons, whatever they expressed even a fleeting interest in. How could it fail? Look at the children's role models: respected professional concert pianist (later to become world famous) and up-and-coming artist (later to become successful and respected) as parents. Under the circumstances, disappointment over mediocrity seems reasonable, even deserved.

The large Victorian-style parlor of my piano teacher's home—the same room in which I dutifully performed my weekly lessons. Chairs set up in semicircle around the piano. I am ten years old. My first piano recital. Mother is there, prophetically wearing black at the death of my childish egotism. Sara fidgeting and making bored faces. Karl, eighteen months older than I, and much more mature, is there to encourage me. He never gloats, never does or says anything that isn't encouraging, which, in its own way, is just as damaging as scorn. Dad sits in the second row of chairs but is so tall and so handsome that he never blends in, his acts of deference pointless but endearing. I am nervous, I suppose, though I remember only two moments—neither could have been more than a millisecond—before and after I play my first piece. In the first instance, I see my little hands poised above the keys and I remember a flash of panic when I realize I don't know where my fingers will go next. In the second moment, after I lift my fingers from the keys at the piece's conclusion, I look at the applauding audience and see Dad's face. There is a beat before he starts clapping and in that beat I see the slightest frown precede his smile. "Frown" is not accurate, really. It is a minute quivering in his face and the suggestion that his mouth is heading for a downturn before it snaps into a smile. But I see it. Whenever I play in his presence after that, I know it's there. I don't ever forget it. My piano playing grows worse the harder I try. I practice and practice until I sprain my hand and eventually quit trying. No one could ever accuse Douglas Van Allen of being unsupportive, yet he did nothing to encourage me after my hand got better. It was, I'm convinced, a relief for him that I seemed to lose interest. Every so often I make another attempt at playing—I doodle on the keys, I take out old exercise books, sometimes I think about private lessons again—but it's always a secret to Dad and the rest of my family. I do it because . . . I'm not sure I can explain why. Is it nostalgia? Is it regret? Or is it because one day I hope to see Dad's face and be sure, be absolutely certain, that nothing preceded his smile?

Yeah, well, when all else fails, blame your parents.

Acclaimed painter Marta Van Allen is best known for her unusual preoccupation with outer space. No other artist working in the photorealistic vein has been as successful painting bits of white and blue and red against a black canvas. But no other artist of her generation has been quite as focused as Van Allen.

Too laudatory

When Marta Van Allen (née Katzenberg) completed the first painting she ever sold (*Starscape 1*), she had been married to famous pianist Douglas Van Allen for twenty-five years, all three of her children had left home for college, career, and what have you, and her husband was in the middle of his busiest year of touring. She had ample time to devote to her art. Having given up serious painting to raise her children, she returned to it with the force and tenacity of some enormous pincered beetle. Once it has bitten something, the only way to make it release its grip is to behead it and slowly, carefully pry the pincers apart.

Karl Van Allen has a terrible secret. Karl—accomplished amateur pianist, honored collegiate athlete, rising young lawyer, handsome husband to Amanda (Amy) née Kenilworth—lovable, unapproachable Karl has a secret he's told to only the people he trusts the most. Legally, Karl's full name is Karl Maria Van Allen. This horrified him as a boy and he insisted Maria be left off all official forms. Only his birth certificate and his passport spoke the truth. Perhaps that's why Karl rarely traveled outside the United States. Karl later grew to understand and appreciate the aristocratic German sound of Karl Maria preceding the strong, stubborn Dutch surname. Though Maria still is not included in his signature or when he is required to supply his full name, the terribleness of his secret is now revealed when he's had too much to drink or when he wants to appear sensitive, intimate, and boyish. At thirty, Karl has no trouble still passing for a boy. It's a large part of his charm.

Sara Van Allen was an overindulged child, perhaps because she was the eldest, the First Child. Whatever she wanted, she got. Whatever talent she seemed about to manifest, she was tutored and directed in. Whenever she changed her mind and embarked on another pursuit, she was lauded, petted, encouraged. Her parents knew that eventually she would settle down and excel, which of course she did. Sara, Sara—sophisticated, mop-top Sara, the curdled voice of a generation. She sits between media-created focus groups and manages to speak to most of them with great success. She has a stinging wit and oodles of charm around everyone but me.

XxXxXx

The Josh Experience

Patrick Von Nella met a man named Josh one day and immediately felt drawn to him. As he talked to this Josh, he thought of another Josh, a former boyfriend of his sister Mara when Mara was fifteen and Patrick was twelve. He loved that Josh with a love that strained a twelve-year-old boy's heart to its breaking point. Patrick and his sister Mara didn't get along, and still don't to this day. Some of the reason why has to do with what happened when Patrick fell in love with Josh and—understanding that Josh would never want to kiss him the way he kissed Mara—used surreptitiously taken photographs to construct an elaborate masturbation fantasy until one day when Mara walked in on him and freaked out.

Josh was photogenic. Film truly captured and sometimes enhanced his beauty. Even though Patrick had taken many pictures of Josh while Josh and Mara were a couple, Patrick had been unable to make it to his thirtieth birthday still possessing a single photograph of his beloved. Somehow every one had disappeared.

Josh had a beautiful prominent nose and wavy hair he just brushed straight back. His hair, light brown like an oiled birch table, fell in perfect disarray. His smile was automatic and spontaneous. His lips, only a little darker than the skin of his face, always looked moist. Patrick wanted Josh's lips to kiss his lips, but knew they lingered on Mara's instead.

But Patrick's twelve-year-old-boy love for Josh wasn't only about Josh's lanky good looks or the disarming freckles on his nose. He and Patrick had so much in common—they both liked to read, they liked the same music (Josh introduced Patrick to his ever-after favorite band, Pink Floyd), the same hairstyle on girls (short and bouncy), and the same TV program (reruns of *The Dick Van Dyke Show*). And Josh was nice to Patrick when few boys were.

Patrick, as a boy, was very interested in photography, and for his twelfth birthday his parents gave him a 35 mm camera and ten rolls of film. He learned to use the camera and began chronicling the daily life of his family. He liked candid portraits of his Mother and Dad together and of his brother Earl and his sister Mara separately. Earl was as photogenic as Josh and had been the subject of a great deal of Patrick's photographs until Josh entered Mara's life and began to spend time with the Von Nella family. Patrick took as many photographs of Josh as he dared. He kept them in a box under his bed and took them out each night, rearranging them, discarding some and adding new ones, until the pictures formed a narrative that Patrick would repeat to himself, embellishing and improvising many times, but never veering too far from the established order of events. As he repeated the story in his thoughts and touched himself, he looked at the pictures.

In his fantasy, Patrick's house has a swimming pool in the backyard and a high privacy fence. Patrick comes home one afternoon and decides to go for a swim. The house is deserted. Patrick takes off his clothes and runs naked through the house and out to the pool. There he finds Josh, wearing a pair of swim trunks, asleep in a lounge chair. Josh has soft, curly hair between his pectorals that continues down his stomach and disappears into the smooth yellow swim trunks. The hairs on his legs are blond. Josh wakes up and grabs Patrick by the shoulders, pulling him close and kissing him feverishly, rhythmically. Patrick then imagines running his hand down Josh's chest.

Patrick would have to admit that he became a reckless masturbator. He wanted to spend as much time as possible with the real Josh and, when Josh was not around, Patrick wanted to spend as much time as he could with his fantasy Josh. One afternoon, when he thought he was alone in the house, he spread his pile of Josh pictures on the family room floor. He drew the drapes, kneeled before the photographs, and placed a towel in front of him. He'd only gotten as far as seeing Josh asleep by the pool when Mara walked in. His back was to her, but it must have been obvious what Patrick was doing.

"What," Mara said, then stopped. Patrick zipped his pants and jumped to his feet. In doing so, he revealed the towel and the spread of photographs, all—Mara noticed—of her boyfriend Josh. She shouted. She didn't use any words. She just shouted. Patrick supposed, when he thought back on that moment over the years, that Mara had meant to scream but anger overcame fear and humiliation overcame disgust. The scream came out a shout. Mara shouted for what seemed like a very long time then left the room. Patrick doesn't think she ever told anyone. He thinks she was too embarrassed. Instead of ruining her brother's life by spreading word of his perversion, Mara broke up with Josh and Patrick never saw him again.

He kept the photographs, but soon his attention turned to other boys and men, his fantasies growing more elaborate with his age. The photographs had vanished, not suddenly but from absentminded neglect. One day, when Patrick hadn't thought about Josh for years, he met a man named Josh, who looked nothing like the other Josh, but who, nonetheless, made Patrick remember his past love. When Patrick got home that day, he looked for a photograph of Josh but couldn't find one. None of them had survived Patrick's many moves. How long ago had the last one been lost? Patrick couldn't say. But Patrick wondered if Mara had destroyed them one day, years ago, when they still all lived together. He wondered if she sneaked into his room and found them. She would have worn gloves and looked through the photographs once, quickly, before taking them with her as she and her teenage friends drove around that night, then went to the park and burned the photographs in the public barbecue pit. They sat around the fire on the concrete benches and shouted obscenities at one another while they laughed. Exactly what they were laughing about none of them could say.

XxXxXx

I've been sitting here just staring at the last sentence I wrote, days ago. I've been staring at it for a minute or more. And suddenly I realized . . . Then, in a blinding flash of illumination . . . As if I'd always known . . . All at once, I understood . . . the problem, the perversity of writing specifically for publication and consumption is that—finally, realistically—there is no epiphany. If you want to comfort, to entertain, to encourage your readers, to be loved and admired, you have to make up a meaning and you have to make it look like you believe it. That's what Sara is so good at, what she's getting away with. Should I admire this? I'd rather write for myself. Fill pages of private, real scribblings that possess, just by existing, all the meaning any writing can have. No moral. No lesson. Why concentrate on creating words and forming them into some structure? Why not just write down everything that happens without trying to edit and make it something it's not? Why not be mundane? Why not write about taking a shit or sitting at a traffic light? Why not why not why not why not

Signed up, at the last possible minute, for group piano class at the university. Why? A) Everyone thinks my novel is a piece of shit. B) I'm not calculating enough to write another one that will please everyone. C) Inside me is something I have to let out, something I have to express. Words won't do it. Photographs won't do it. Art won't do it. So I come back to music once again. Music has never gone away. Music is inside me. I know it. I'm a Van Allen. I'm the son of Douglas Fucking Van Allen. But why is it taking me so long to reach my potential? Mother says I don't apply myself. Dad's advice was always to "focus." But it's more difficult than that, more complicated. The privileged, the talented think it's easy because it was for them. Because they're special. Because they were born to it. Well, I'm proof that sometimes you have to earn it. Sometimes, in spite of your environment, you have to prove you're worthy. And I have to be worthy. I have to believe. I have to. I just have to.

Friday

Can't sleep, so I'll write it all down. We left home late even though I had taken the day off from work. The drive to the cabin takes five hours on a good day, which is why we only go up there on special occasions and long weekends. For Karl and Amy, the drive is just two hours, so they're there most weekends into the fall. "Cabin" is a rather affected way of referring to a vacation home set in the woods near a state forest preserve. Like the other homes there, Karl's place is a massive, wooden A-frame that can't be seen from the winding road. Two floors and five bedrooms—perfect for entertaining. Paul didn't get home from giving his piano lessons until four and it was just after six by the time we merged onto the interstate. I tried not to be pissed. It wouldn't have bothered me if we had stayed home. Leaving late just meant we'd be tired and cranky when we arrived and that we'd have to put up with perpetually chirpy Amy. I think I'm the only person who doesn't just adore her and I'm not even sure why I feel this way. Let me rephrase that—I'm not sure there's a rational reason for the way I feel. I first met her when Karl brought her home for a big Thanksgiving get-together. This was before I met Paul and when I had just broken up with Gerald the asshole, so just the idea of someone in a relationship was enough to make me cynical. Of course, this wasn't just anyone; this was Karl. Was it because she seemed to fit right in, like she was preordained to be part of the family? Mother sparkled and Dad flirted. Even Sara reigned in her usual world-weary barbs. How could you not like a woman who even Sara seemed to respect? A woman so attractive, so well mannered, so seemingly perfect for my seemingly perfect brother? During dinner the first night we met, Amy leaned over to me and whispered, "Karl's told me so much about you. You're lucky to be so close to your brother." I'm sure I smiled politely, but I was embarrassed and mortified because I knew just by her tone of voice that they had not only had sex but would be married. Whenever she smiled at me or spoke to me that night, I responded appropriately, but privately I wanted to mess up her hair, see a look of shock and disappointment come across her face. It was a nice drive up to the cabin, actually. After three hours, Paul took over driving, and I pulled out some sandwiches from the portable cooler. We played a tape of Rachmaninoff piano pieces, munched the sandwiches, and talked about Paul's piano students and my lawyers. For a while, my ambivalence vanished as the sun dropped closer to the horizon and the highway pulled us along. They were waiting up for us when we arrived around 11:30. Karl looked tired, his smile a little lopsided and his eyelids heavy. Amy brought out a cheese platter and poured us a little wine. Karl had to ask the inevitable: "What's up with the law firm, Mikey?" and did I ever look into that paralegal program at the community college? Paul and Amy were chattering away, catching up like two sorority girls who hadn't seen each other since graduation. I must have rolled my eyes because Karl gave me one of his exasperated, endearing grins and promised not to nag. So then Amy said, "That's right. It's a holiday. No talking about labor. No shop talk and no nagging." Amy thinks Karl and I talk shop whenever my job comes up, as though our positions at law firms are linked by anything other than the mutual contempt lawyers and support staff have for each other. I was just about to speak when Paul shot me one of his don't-be-a-prick looks. "I'm beat," I said with a fake yawn and we all go to bed. Paul was asleep seconds after lying down, but I'm still wide awake, scribbling, scribbling, scribbling.

Saturday

Up late again and, just like yesterday, I'm going to try and put it all down on paper precisely because nothing happened. In fact, I tried hard to relax and have a good time today and, remarkably, I succeeded. I just get so wound up with work and day-to-day stuff that for a little while—until the trees and the lazy routine start weaving their spell on me—I carry all that tension, resentment, and impatience here with me. Sometimes I just have to stand on the deck, sip some freshly brewed coffee, feel the sun on my face, and remember to breathe—in . . . out . . . in . . . out—a few times and, with the help of the fresh air and bright green leaves that rustle just a bit in the imperceptible breeze, everything unpleasant seems so distant. Today went by quickly. I slept until ten and I remember Paul getting up—it must have been seven or eight—but I went right back to sleep. When I did wake up, I could hear Karl and Amy and Paul talking downstairs. The words weren't distinct, but every so often they laughed and the steady sound of unintelligible conversation was comforting. Amy had decorated the guest rooms as if they were in a bed-and-breakfast—chenille bedspreads, washbowls and washbowl stands, dark wood barley-twist furniture, lacy curtains. Sometimes the whole look was oppressive and fake, but this morning in bed I saw the light filtering through the sheer curtains and smelled a strange mix of coffee and jasmine. A sense of peace came over me like a paralysis. I just lay there until past eleven—listening, smelling, looking. "You must have been really tired," Amy said to me when I finally came downstairs into the kitchen portion of the great room. She had coffee ready and toast and cereal. She offered to make eggs for me, but I told her not to bother. What must it be like, I wondered, looking at my sister-in-law, to be so naturally, unabashedly, goddamned nice? And why, I asked myself, as she hummed around the kitchen, cleaning up the last of the breakfast dishes, couldn't I like her? Did I require a certain amount of deviousness, a splash of perversion, some character flaw before I ended up liking someone? I decided I would try, really try to reach some sort of one-sided truce with her. Since she seemed to genuinely like me, I would find something to genuinely like about her. She saw me smile and smiled back as she started packing apples in a backpack. Karl was in the living-room area and asked if I was ready for a hike. Paul was sitting at the grand piano, playing it very quietly with his left hand. "Let me finish my coffee first," I said. Instead of sounding jovial, the words came out in a whine. "You coming with, Paul?" Karl asked, clapping his hands on Paul's shoulder and giving him a good-natured massage. Paul brought his right hand up to the keyboard and continued playing. I think Paul is attracted to Karl (and who wouldn't be). "Amy and I are going mushroom hunting," Paul said, storming into several bars from Barber's Piano Sonata, then stopping. "We'll start out with you, anyway."

"Go up through the glade to the mound," Karl said to Paul, then turned toward Amy in the kitchen area. "That's the best place, isn't it?" For a minute, I thought I'd stepped into some weird version of a Chekhov play. And then I thought—*Hey, I'm trusting that Amy won't gather poison mushrooms, which if you look at it isn't that different from trusting a sushi chef to use only fresh, parasite-free seafood.* I certainly knew Amy better than any sushi chef. Item number one on my new "Reasons to Like Amy" list—I can trust her not to poison me. So the four of us started off before lunch—Karl in the lead wearing cutoff shorts, thin T-shirt, his ancient hiking boots, and the backpack full of bottled water, fruit, and a first-aid kit. Karl, despite all appearances, never was in Cub Scouts or Boy Scouts or any Scouts. He just knows all that stuff—born to it naturally as he was born to his intelligence, his athletic good looks, his musical talent, and his dedication to interpreting the law while making lots of money. His ease of accomplishment in everything started to rub against my decision to have a good day. But then he turned around to talk to Amy and Paul, who dawdled behind with baskets, and he smiled when he spoke and it seemed fitting he was so gifted. Who better? Item number two on my Amy list—Karl loves her. The rightness of Karl's actions has to extend to his choice of a partner. Karl and I picked our way around some mossy boulders. Paul and Amy laughed from somewhere, but I couldn't tell how far away they were now. The birch trees and the pines obscured them as Karl and I continued up to the ridge. He asked me if I was going home for Dad's recital. I told him, "Probably." "You're just keeping Mom in suspense," Karl said and I replied, "Objection. Circumstantial evidence." Then he tells me that Dad is pretty nervous about the recital and doesn't it seem funny he'd be nervous about anything anymore. I told Karl I couldn't stand the way Mother mentioned her opening only in passing. I told him I thought she was being egregiously self-effacing and too obvious. Karl just sighed and stopped to look at a lone wildflower that grew out of a crevice between two large rocks. "It never occurred to you that she's genuinely more excited about Dad's recital? She always is," he said. We walked without speaking for several minutes and then I blurted out, "Why is it such a big deal for him?" I'm the one who always breaks our silences it seems. "He's played this guy before. He's even recorded him."

So then Karl has to lecture me: "Have you ever heard any of Scriabin's sonatas? They're difficult even for pianists of Dad's stature. So many people think of Scriabin and Horowitz in the same breath. It must be hard to live up to everyone's expectations, and not all the reviews of Dad's Scriabin CD were glowing. Plus there's a big difference between playing preludes and études and playing a sonata. You should know that." Now it was my turn to sigh. "Yeah, sonatas are longer," I said. Karl just looks at me with those blue eyes and says, "It would mean a lot to him if we were all there. He's getting older, maybe a little insecure. Would it kill you to be there?" I told him I'd have to see if I had enough vacation but that I would probably be there. Sometimes I think Karl can convince me to agree to anything. Then he asks if Paul will come too and I tell him probably not. It's too close to the end of the semester. "Understandable but unfortunate," he said. "Mom and Dad don't get to see him much. They should spend more time with the two of you." *They should spend more time with each other,* I thought and then replied sarcastically, "Paul makes Mother uncomfortable and vice versa. There are two kinds of mother-gay son relationships—close and intimate or strained and uncomfortable. Guess which cliché applies." Karl tipped his head toward me a little. "It would mean a lot to Dad if we were all there," he said. The rest of the hike was beautiful and quiet. Karl seemed to be enjoying the woods and the climb as much as I was, so we rarely spoke. When we reached the ridge, I could see two people far below in a clearing. Sure it was Paul and Amy, I cupped my hands to my mouth and shouted Paul's name. The word echoed around us and then faded into the August heat. I saw Paul wave and seem to shout, but the sound never made it up to us. "Let's go," Karl said, touching me on the shoulder. A chill ran up my spine, even though I was sweating from the climb.

And so our days go here. A little exercise, food, conversation, rest, and piano playing. Karl and Amy always ask Paul to play and today was no different. But before dinner, Paul and I were helping Amy in the kitchen and Karl was at the piano. I could hear him. There was a lot of beauty and elegance even in his doodling, which made me sad. I'd been chattering along with Paul and Amy until Karl started, then I became quiet and listened. He was playing a stormy, dramatic piece I'd never heard before, launching into clusters of fat, swirling chords that barely let up until the end. I asked Paul what the piece was. He shrugged and raised his voice so Karl could hear. "That's an awfully bold piece for a nonprofessional to play," Paul said. Karl stuck his head into the kitchen. "Scriabin," he said. "One of the études. Opus 42, Number 5. It's on Dad's CD. Aren't I presumptuous?" He laughed. "I should know that," Paul said, a little embarrassed, but so graceful about it. I just glared at Karl. A setup. That fucking recital. "It's such a beautiful piece. Strange, but beautiful," Amy said, as if she would even know. So I said, with only a little sarcasm, "You play it so well. Maybe you should perform at the recital instead of Dad." And Karl laughed again. This time Paul glared at me. After everyone was asleep, I went downstairs and scanned the bookshelves for a music encyclopedia. I guess I have to face the fact that Karl can always motivate me, even if it's only to keep up with him. Under S, this is what I found:

Alexander Nikolaievich Scriabin (1872-1915). Russian composer and pianist best known for ten piano sonatas and four large-scale symphonic works, including *Le Poème de l'extase* (1904). Scriabin is unique in the annals of Russian music for his refusal to use traditional folk songs and rhythms. Instead, Scriabin created his own tonal system that embodied a bizarre patchwork of philosophical beliefs he derived from Theosophy and Hinduism. Highly regarded in Russia, where he is considered Chopin's equal, Scriabin was dismissed as a novelty in the West until recently when renewed interest in his piano compositions created a small flood of performances and recordings.

What the hell is Theosophy?

Can't sleep again, which is bad on a weeknight. I'll be a wreck at work tomorrow, but considering how little I'm paid and how mindless the job is, I guess it doesn't matter. What matters is why I can't sleep—Scriabin. It's funny to think that four days ago I'd barely heard of him . . . and now I'm hooked. Let me back up and lay it all out. Sunday was pretty lazy, though Karl managed to drag us out for another hike. He drives me crazy sometimes. There are times when I just want to get away from him, leave him and his perfect wife and his perfect looks and all his fucking effortlessness way, way behind me. Then I have this rush of remorse for thinking anything bad and I try to be happy for him. For example: Sunday on the hike, I was walking with Paul and we were behind Karl and Amy. At first, I was fine. It was cooler than Saturday, just about perfect weather. The trees, the slight breeze, the sunshine, the bird calls—it was so peaceful. We were quiet, enjoying our last taste of this before heading back to our weekday lives. Everything seemed right. It really did. I had the sense that all the choices I'd made in my life were for the best, that all my disappointments were trivial, that being able to walk in the woods with someone I loved was what mattered. It was a trick, of course. A fucking trick. I saw Karl reach over and take Amy's hand in a natural and tender movement and all my illusions collapsed. If Paul had held my hand at that moment, it would have felt false. For just a second, I hated Karl and Amy. I hated the fact that they had a vacation home and money and health and good looks and everything. I hated Paul because he wasn't perfect, because his imperfections had been revealed to me over the course of our three years together. I hated the sun for shining, hated the day for looking so beautiful when I knew the ozone layer was being destroyed and that we were all developing skin cancer. Then the hatred passed and I was just pathetic. On the drive home we didn't talk much. I was still depressed from the walk and Paul knew enough just to ignore me, knew that my famous undirected anger might come spewing out at him just because he was there. But as the drive progressed, I began to feel guilty. I looked at Paul's profile as he drove and remembered why I loved him. As always, he knew I was watching him. "What are you looking at?" he asked, not taking his eyes off the road. His tone was cautious, but optimistic. Maybe he thought I was glaring instead of admiring him. "Your nose, your hair," I said, then added, "how handsome you are in the fading light," with a touch of silly melodrama to lighten the mood. "OK, so now I'm only handsome in low light," he said and turned quickly toward me to smile. I said, "I can be such an asshole sometimes." And he said, "Sometimes?" Again the smile, this time as he watched the road. I wanted to explain everything, so I blurted out stuff about unresolved childhood issues and being around my family, to which he replied, "Oh, please. First of all, your moods are not confined to visits with your family. Second, Karl and Amy are never anything but gracious hosts. I've heard all your stories about parental wrongdoing and filial competition, but all I ever see when we actually visit your brother is how much he loves you." I could either try to explain or I could acquiesce. When I write things down, they seem to make so much sense, yet nothing I could say to Paul would make him understand. Even if I read him this journal, I know all my arguments would evaporate with one terribly logical remark or an exasperated look from him. "I wish I could explain," I said, genuinely sad. "It's just that he has everything and everything comes to him so easily. Sometimes it makes me angry." Paul said I was being ridiculous and that I'd put Karl up on a pedestal. "He's a pretty wonderful guy," Paul said, "but he's not perfect and he's not you. The way you and Karl acted and interacted when you were kids is one thing, but you're grown-ups now. It can't still be competition—he's a lawyer, he's married, he's heterosexual. You don't want to be a lawyer. You don't want to be straight. You're as good as married." Paul reached over and took my hand. "Am I missing something?"

"No," I said. It just wasn't worth the effort to explain. "I love Karl."

"How could anyone not love Karl?" Paul said, and I got a horrible, dizzying feeling.

"Right," I said very quietly, and then, after a bit, so Paul wouldn't think his words and my action were related, I moved my hand away.

This morning I woke up, ready for everything to be different. Maybe it was the unavoidable sense of starting over you have after a holiday. I went back to work convinced that as of today I would start being a better employee, a better companion and lover, a better brother, a better son. Keeping this feeling isn't easy when you work at Highsmith, Ripley, and Rendell. If I were a lawyer or a paralegal or even a secretary, things might be easier. But I'm on the bottom rung here—a file clerk. It pains me to go into the details of my job. All day long I categorize depositions and reports and letters and other legal documents, pasting color-coded numbers and letters onto the manila folders and then filing them in an enormous room of rolling shelves. Most days I have a stack of new documents to prepare, categorize, and file. Today, even though it was after a holiday, the stack was larger than usual. This wouldn't be half so bad, mindless, pretty easy work, except the lawyers treat me like some subhuman life-form—never speaking directly to me and always going through my boss. They come in all slick and well groomed, smelling of starch and cologne, and don't even look at me. "Barbara," they'll say to my boss, "I need the McLintock depositions by this afternoon." Once they've left, Barbara very nicely comes over and asks for the files. She supervises, but she doesn't know where everything is like I do. The rolling shelves are my domain; I can picture where certain files are in my head. "McLintock," I might say, "Seven eighty-two. The depositions are on the third shelf down on the far left." If those assholes would just ask me, I could walk over and place the file in their manicured hands and save them twenty minutes. A lot of the male lawyers are young and handsome in a way that makes you angry for finding them attractive. If I worked at Karl's firm and wasn't his brother, I bet he'd treat me the same way. Despite all this, I came to work ready to be a better file clerk. The morning was easy to get through because I had decided last night to shop at Kendall's and buy a CD of Horowitz playing Scriabin. The description of Scriabin and his work I'd read made me curious. I expected bizarre, exotic music, of which the étude Karl had played was only a warm-up. Add to that the fact that Dad was nervous about performing one of the sonatas and I knew I had to hear the competition. All I could find was a compilation disc with two sonatas, a lot of preludes and a few études, including the one Karl had played—Opus 42, Number 5. The rest of the day, the CD sat in a bag in my backpack on the floor by my desk. When the day got too boring or irritating, I'd just look at my backpack and I could hear a few bars of the wild, dramatic étude. I got home at six. I knew Paul had class, so I'd have the apartment to myself. I popped the disc into the player and waited for the Piano Sonata Number 5, Opus 53 to begin. I was completely unprepared for what came next. At first, the piano growled and trembled, then abruptly turned to slow, soft musings that built into a jaunty gallop and crashed to a shimmering, pounding crescendo. The musing returned, but there was a sadness and resignation in it now that I hadn't heard the first time. Again and again waves of sound came and went, an aching melody trying to break out of chaos. The structure seemed to repeat, yet each time it was different, sucking me into a terrifying and beautiful vortex of sound, circling around a theme but never landing on it. Striving and yearning, pushing and falling back, then rising again, crashing and galloping and crashing again, up and up into a whirling, pounding, discordant crescendo that abruptly stopped as if the pianist had been flung far into space. The music had ended, but I could hear it echoing until the first few notes of the next piece began. I stopped the CD and just sat there for a moment to take in what I'd heard. Then I played the sonata again, this time trying to read the liner notes, but only picked out disconnected phrases as the music took my attention: impetuoso con stravaganza, languido, accacezzevole, estatico. When the sonata finished the second time, I stopped the CD and read the poem Scriabin had written to go with the piece:

> I summon you to life, secret yearnings!
> You who have been drowned in the dark depths
> Of the creative spirit, you timorous
> Embryos of life, it is to you that I bring daring.

The notes said it was an excerpt from a longer "erotic-philosophical" poem called "Poem of Ecstasy," which was also the name of a symphonic piece by Scriabin. The notes also described the climax of the sonata as "orgiastic," which didn't seem quite right to me, and mentioned a "mystic" or "Promethean" chord used in the sonata, a chord which Scriabin apparently invented. I had no idea you could invent a chord. I thought they just existed for all to use. Over at the piano, I propped up the liner notes. C, F-sharp, B-flat, E, A, D. I played the notes separately, tentatively—three with my right hand and three with my left—each echoing for a second before the next came. Then, softly, I played them as one. The sound was brutal, discordant, and I recognized it from the sonata. Now that my fingers were positioned, I brought them down with determination. The chord clanged, more savage than mystic. Before the notes faded, I played the chord again, much louder this time, banging the keys over and over wildly as if I was an overwrought pianist reaching the climax of his performance. Then I stopped and let the sound evaporate. At that moment, as the air around me settled back into the mundane, I became so sad. It wasn't a melancholy sadness or the kind of sadness that brings tears. It was as if my place in a vast and infinite universe had become clear, revealing how small I was, how insignificant my life had been. Almost one hundred years ago, Scriabin wrote this sonata and somehow, over time and space, I received it, took it in, and was changed by it. Horowitz had played it, adding to it and making it real. Recording engineers had tweaked and fiddled to make sure it sounded perfect. Someone had built the piano; someone else designed the CD cover. All had contributed. Yet what had I done? Merely listened, consumed the music, then I'd go about my daily routine, thinking I was changed, thinking things were different now, when, in fact, everything was exactly as it had been. The light in the apartment was fading as the days grew shorter. September would turn into October, then another year would go by, and I would still have done nothing. I listened to the sonata again. This time, a story began to unfold—not just a series of beautiful, eerie, amazing notes and chords but a meaning. The music spoke to me, showed me that creativity has its source in the soul and that it strives to overcome the mundane and break out into the swirling chaos of the infinite. I could hear this! And what it told me was to keep striving. To struggle and create. To unleash what's chained inside me. Suddenly, my decision to study music again became not some ridiculous attempt to compete with Dad or Paul or Karl. It was the obvious next step in my evolution. Instead of being frightened by the chaos, I need to embrace it, to step into the maelstrom of sound and energy and life that whirled around me. Whereas before I thought this would destroy me, tear me apart, now I understood that only by giving in and joining this would I achieve what I desire.

It's late now—2 a.m.—and I've been scribbling for hours. I went to bed with Paul at eleven but couldn't fall asleep, my mind racing with thoughts of what's ahead. So I got up, put on the headphones, and listened to the Scriabin CD all the way through. Many beautiful pieces and another amazing sonata—Number 3, called "Soul States." Still the Fifth Sonata has cast its spell over me. My discovery of it seems prophetic given my new attempt at piano lessons. To be able to play this music instead of just listening to it, to be a part of its creation and re-creation is a lofty goal but so fitting. The plan: start by playing the smaller pieces and work my way up to the Fifth Sonata. But not for an audience! For myself. This is the way. I feel it. This frightening and glorious music is what I've been looking for. With it inside me, with it directing my fingers, hands, body, I'll be alive. Really, truly alive—

I need to find out more about Scriabin and his philosophy, which, hopefully, I'll be able to understand, since philosophy is not my strong point. Piano lessons start on Thursday. I'm still not tired, though I will be this afternoon when work is at its most dreary. Tonight, I'll sleep and maybe dream of music.

XxXxXx

Alexander Nikolaievich Scriabin—born Moscow on Christmas Day 1871 (Jan. 6, 1872, in New Style calendar)—believed there was a mystical connection between him and Christ—died Moscow April 27, 1915, of gangrene resulting from an infected pimple on his upper lip.

"I met Scriabin in 1896 when I was only fifteen years old, and I was struck by his frail appearance, his extreme nervousness. I saw him again in 1902, when he was already a professor at the Moscow Conservatory, a husband and a father, and at that meeting, too, he possessed a strange tenderness in his bearing, a curious childishness in his manner."

Boris de Schloezer (music critic and friend of Scriabin's)

XxXxXx

Names of some of his piano pieces

Poème Satanique
Poème Fantastique
Quasi-Valse
Rêverie
Fragilité
Wingèd Poem (Poème Ailé)
Dance of Languor (Danse Languide)
Enigma
Desire
Danced Caress (Caresse Dansée)
Dreaming (En Rêvant)
Toward the Flame (Vers le Flamme)
Poème-Nocturne
Dark Flames (Flammes Sombres)
Poème Tragique

Main Orchestral Works

Op. 20—Piano Concerto, F# minor (1896-1897)
Op. 26—Symphony No. 1, E major with chorus (1899-1900)
Op. 29—Symphony No. 2, C minor (1901)
Op. 43—Symphony No. 3, "The Divine Poem" (1903-1904)
Op. 54—"The Poem of Ecstasy" (1905-1907)
Op. 60—*Prometheus*, "The Poem of Fire" (1909-1910)

XxXxXx

Went to library at lunch and found Scriabin biography and short book on his philosophy. Only read parts of it, so need to study this further.

More than anything, Scriabin wanted his music to transform the world and its inhabitants—transubstantiation—sound into ecstasy.

Ecstasy = joy of unrestrained creative activity

Universe (the Spirit) is eternal creation with no outward aim or motive—a divine play with worlds.

Creating Spirit—the Universe at play—the Creating Spirit does not realize absolute value of creation—it has subjected itself to a purpose and made activity a means toward another end.

The faster the pulse of life beats in the Universe, the faster its rhythm becomes and the clearer it becomes that the Spirit is creation alone—an end in itself.

Life = Play

When the Spirit, reaching the climax of its activity, which is bit by bit tearing it away from the delusions of utility and relativity, comprehends the unrestrained activity, its very substance—Ecstasy will arise.

At first, Scriabin deified this Spirit, but later he asserted himself as the source of the power.

And this amazing, weird, sad, triumphant excerpt from Scriabin's notebooks around 1903-1905, at the time he was writing his symphonic poem "Poem of Ecstasy" and just before writing the Fifth Sonata:

> I yearn for the new and the unknown. I want to create, create consciously. I want to ascend the summit. I want to enthrall the world by my creative work, by its wondrous beauty. I want to be the brightest imaginable light, the largest sun. I want to illuminate the universe by my light. I want to engulf everything and absorb everything in my individuality. I want to give delight to the world. I want to take the world as one takes a lover . . .
>   I create the infinite future, the repose in me, the sorrow and joy in me. I am nothing. I am what I create. The destiny of the Universe is clear. I have a will to live. I love life. I am God. I am nothing. I want to be all. I have generated my antithesis—time, space, and plurality. This antithesis is myself; for I am only what I engender. I want to be

God. I want to return to myself. The world seeks God. I seek myself. The world is yearning for God. I am yearning for myself. I am the world. I am the search for God, for I am only what I seek. The history of human consciousness begins with my search and with my return.

Also in this book is a photograph of Scriabin, taken in Paris in 1905 when he was thirty-four, though he looks younger. It is of his face and shoulders. He's in profile (his right side), looking slightly upward. The lower half of his face—covered by a bushy mustache and Vandyke—almost blends into the background, but above that is a beautiful nose, remarkably straight, and the unblemished, luminescent skin of his forehead and cheeks. His hair is full, brushed back and just coming over a high, starched collar. I imagine his hair is brown and I think I see touches of gray. He seems quite small—despite anything in the picture to compare him to—his eyebrow thin and not reaching the corner of his eye. He seems lost in thought and quite handsome. The caption says it was his favorite photograph of himself, which he frequently gave to admirers. I photocopied it. To his intimates, he was known as Sasha.

2

I have to stop reading. My head is heavy with facts, loaded with answers and questions.

It would be so easy if these pages brought recollection, like a key turning in a rusty lock with a click. A screech of hinges. The door bangs open and the other side is my former life, illuminated by the sun like some secret garden.

Instead, I wonder if this could be an elaborate trick. Could someone have copied my handwriting and made this up? I remember nothing of this life, though the people are clear enough.

The apartment is quiet with just the street noise as an ever-present accompaniment. How long ago did the music from the CD player stop? The bedroom seems brighter and I notice that I can no longer hear the rain. There is sunlight penetrating the light well, revealing the peeling paint on the exterior walls, illuminating the puddles of rainwater and rotting leaves in the corners. I hear dripping, slow and persistent.

What a sad person I was. Is that why I ended up in the hospital? Has all that been erased, or will it slowly reappear—a nasty comment here, an inconsiderate action there—until I am Mike again? The old Mike. The Mike who can't sleep. And Sasha, poor Sasha. Dead for so long. Dead and crazy. But he's gone now, which must mean I'm cured. He had lingered on like an echo, amplified temporarily by the drugs, perhaps, and finally faded away.

I stand up and take the notebook with me into the living room. The evidence of my old life must be in the apartment somewhere. I check the spines of compact discs that are stacked on the floor by the CD player and neatly arranged on shelves against the wall. I look for the word *Scriabin,* knowing it will leap out at me. I run my index finger along each spine, cock my head so I can read better, and wait for some reaction. There should be at least two Scriabin CDs—Horowitz and Dad—but I find neither. I start again, sure that the jumble of sideways letters have masked the pattern I seek.

Again, nothing.

I look around the living room for stray CDs, for drawers I haven't opened, for places things might be hidden or discarded. When I'm done with the living room, I start in the bedroom, open each box in the closet, feel inside the mattress, lift up clothing in drawers.

Still nothing. And I'm exhausted. I go out to the living room once more, barely make it to the couch by the window. My hands are shaking and my left eyelid twiches. I have to reach up and press my palm against my eyebrow to make it stop. My heart pounds, my breathing is erratic. I look at the street, watch the people as they hurry by. The sun is behind another cloud. The rain begins to fall, lightly.

It could all be made up. If I wrote the journal why would I have to tell the truth? If I was crazy, why should I believe anything I wrote? Yet the old Mike—the journal Mike—doesn't sound crazy at all. Just lost.

The phone rings and I shout—an involuntary *Ah!* as if the ringing had forced air from my lungs. Then I think *No,* as the phone rings again, *No.* It rings a third time, daring me. Then a final ring. As the clanging of the bell fades away, I recognize, quite clearly, that the ringer's tone is a C.

I hum the note, then go to the piano and try random keys until I hear it. I pound the key several times and hum. C. C. C. C. C. What were the other notes of that chord? I retrieve the notebook from the couch and flip though the early pages until I find it: the mystic chord. C, F-sharp, B-flat, E, A, D. For a moment, I think I've unlocked the piano's mysteries. If this key is C, then the next white key at the beginning of a group of three black keys must also be a C. A and B would come before C and, since there are only four white keys separating one C from another, the black keys don't have letters. They are the sharps and the flats.

The speed with which I figure this out makes me think I've remembered it, even though there is no flash of recognition, but I begin to doubt. How do I tell a sharp from a flat? How can I be sure a C is really a C? I scan the books on the piano's music rest, but they are all scores and assume familiarity. As with so many things I've encountered, it seems, explanations of the basic things are the most difficult to find.

I play the C again, listfully, then return to my reading.

Thursday

Just after midnight. Brain will not shut down. Piano class starts today and I'm pretty nervous. To make things worse, Mother called today. Here's the blow by blow with subtext provided in parentheses:

The phone rings.

ME: Hello?

MOTHER: (brightly) You're there. What a surprise! (Ah hah! You thought you could avoid me indefinitely.)

ME: Hello, Mother.

MOTHER: I just got off the phone with Karl and Amy. It sounds like you had a wonderful time. (Notice that I didn't say "you and Paul." If I don't mention him, maybe he'll go away. Not that I have anything against him. It's the idea of the two of you as a couple that I refuse to acknowledge. Call me old fashioned. Call me a bigot. Go ahead. You may as well. I know that's what you're thinking. As I've told you, I have no moral issue with your life-style. Your father and I know many gay men—the music and art world being what it is—and we've even had male couples over for dinner—you remember your father's friend Christian and his series of "partners." None of them lasted more than two years. That's what disturbs me, Michael—the impermanence, the hedonism. As soon as things become challenging or as soon as some pretty boy bats his eyes, it's over. I've seen it so many times. You've experienced it as well. Wasn't his name Gerald? And that's only the one I know about. So you and Paul have been together for three years. My congratulations. Your father and I have been married for almost forty years and have the three of you. What will you have when you're my age? A house full of cats and pornographic magazines.) You should have told me you were going up to the cabin. (But that would mean you'd actually have to call me on your own.)

ME: Well, it was sort of last minute. We weren't sure if Paul could get away. Classes started this week and his first recital is scheduled for the end of the month. (Paul. PAUL. Go ahead. Ask me what he's playing. Ask me how he is. Ask me how we're getting along. I dare you. You're not old fashioned, just ignorant and stubborn. You always bring up Christian as if he's the only fag you know. Christian Hannaran is a pig with money. Nobody could stand being with him for more than a year. He's prissy, conceited, and I happen to know that he holds interviews when he needs a new boyfriend. Interviews! With a series of questions about fashion sense and sexual habits followed by a nude modeling session.)

MOTHER: Karl tells me you'll be able to make your father's big recital in November. He'll be so happy. We haven't seen all three of you together since Christmas last year. (Notice that I'm not mentioning my opening. I don't expect everyone to be as interested in that as in your father's recital. He's the important one. Still, I do get good reviews and sales, so your support and encouragement, although always hoped for, isn't necessary. It's not as if you really know anything about painting anyway.)

ME: (sharply) I told Karl I'd *probably* be there. I have to see about vacation time.

MOTHER: Surely a day or two won't be a problem. (You can make all the excuses you want and I'll shoot them down. I don't care that you'd rather not be here to make your father and me happy. I'm just asking you for four days. Considering how much we've done for you, I think that's a trifle. But then, you've always been ungrateful, even hurtful, when it comes to your family. It isn't like you have a career to keep you from coming home. Surely a law firm can survive without a file clerk for two days.)

ME: (a little desperate) It's not just work. I have school too. (Oh, shit.)

MOTHER: (brightly) School? (I hope you've finally taken our advice and enrolled in that paralegal studies program Karl recommended. Since it's unlikely you'll ever be married, you don't need much money, but you'll have to do better than file clerk. Do you still want to be a file clerk when you're thirty-five? Wouldn't that be more than a little embarrassing?) I didn't know you were taking classes again.

ME: Just one class, Mother. But with work and school, it won't be so easy to get away. (Change the subject. Quick!) So where's Dad this week?

MOTHER: San Francisco, I think. The Brahms Second. (Oh no, you don't.) What class are you taking? Something fun or something serious?

ME: I thought Dad wasn't doing the Brahms this year. What happened to expanding his repertoire? Hey, isn't your opening coming up?

MOTHER: (trying to temper her delight at my asking) Oh, don't remind me! There's still so much to do. It's the Friday before your father's recital, you know. So there's another reason for you to come home for a few days. (Michael, you're evading the question, which means you're not taking paralegal studies and instead are off on one of your wild goose chases. Well, what is it this time? Filmmaking? Sculpture? Furniture design? Michael, you're twenty-nine years old. If you had any real artistic talent, don't you think it would have manifested itself by now? Sometimes I think the only real talent you have is for fooling yourself.) You didn't say what class you're taking.

ME: (disingenuously) Oh, I thought I'd brush up on my piano skills. (Go ahead. Just get it over with. Tell me how ridiculous I am and how I'm only making yet another pathetic attempt to be like Dad and Karl. Well, you're wrong. You're so wrong this time. I'm doing this for myself, for my personal growth, and I don't care what you think.)

MOTHER: How nice! Well, it's certainly been a long time since you last played, hasn't it? At least twenty years, I would think—right before you hurt your hand. (Well, it could have been worse. At least you're not trying to prove something or embark on some new, unrealistic "career.") I'm sure it's like riding a bicycle, dear. Not that I know anything about piano playing. (Nor do you, since I doubt very much that you've touched a piano in twenty years. But you are my son and I love you, so I'll be as encouraging as I can.)

ME: (trying not to sound defensive) I still play occasionally. We have a piano, you know. (Remember that I live and have sex with a piano-playing man named Paul. Paul. Paul. Paul.)

MOTHER: Of course you do, Michael. We're a very musical family. (All except for you. It hardly seems possible that you could be less musical than you are.)

ME: (unable to resist being a little snide) Thanks for your support, Mother. [Mother sighs. Long pause.]

MOTHER: Michael, what's the matter? (Besides your usual anger and frustration? I'm sure that you've pinned whatever it is on me, your evil mother who can't possibly do anything right. Well, what can I expect? I suppose it's too much to ask that all three of my children be reasonable.)

ME: (petulantly) Nothing's the matter. (Why should I expect you to have any consideration for my feelings? Why should I think you'd understand what it's like to be the one everyone pities for being untalented? Well, I don't care what you or Dad or Sara or Karl thinks anymore. I don't. I really don't.)

MOTHER: (concerned but a bit exasperated) Are you depressed again? You know Dr. Jamison will write you a prescription any time. I'm sure he can recommend someone near you. Shall I call him?

ME: (biting down on each word) I'm. Not. Depressed. I don't need any pills, Mother. I'm just taking a piano class, for God's sake. What's the big deal? You're blowing it all out of proportion as usual.

MOTHER: Michael, I called to see if you were coming home for your father's recital. As usual, you've turned the conversation into some sort of argument. I'm sorry if I've upset you, though I really don't know what I said to provoke you.

ME: It doesn't matter. (Whatever I would say now would just be turned around so it's my fault, my problem, anyway. I should just hang up.) [Long pause]

MOTHER: Well, when do you think you'll know about your vacation time?

ME: I'll ask tomorrow. I'll find out Paul's schedule tonight.

MOTHER: Let me know as soon as you can. (I suppose it's inevitable you'll bring him.)

ME: Yeah. Gotta go. Bye.

Is it any wonder I'm so freaked out about starting class today? I'll be hearing Mother and Dad in my head, seeing their looks of pity and indulgence. Sara's look of scorn and superiority. Karl's eyes telling me to keeping trying and telling me to believe in myself. So easy for him. So easy.

XxXxXx

More about Scriabin

Scriabin was synaesthetic—he heard colors. He wrote a part for a "keyboard of light" in his last major completed work, *Prometheus, Poem of Fire.* The clavier à lumière was to be a device that bathed the concert hall in a complicated choreography of colored light. The instrument never really existed and the piece was never performed as he envisioned it. What would it be like to be synaesthetic? How does that happen? For Scriabin, different pitches represented specific colors—C was an intense red, G was orange, D was yellow, and so on. Each pitch and color was also associated with a sensation or philosophical element—red for human will, orange for creative play, yellow for joy. . . . It's a mystery to me. Can you develop this sense? I listen to the Fifth Sonata and I'm swept up in an indescribable series of emotions, my mind imagining scenes and movement but no color. I play a C on the piano and I can think "red" because I'm told red = C, but it's artificial. My mind is too cluttered with expectation. I have to let go. I have to free it of all associations and just hear the music. But how? When?

Two Weird Similarities Between Me and Scriabin

1. Scriabin injured his left hand when he was twenty-one from over-practicing.
2. Scriabin was probably sexually attracted to men, though he repressed it and overcompensated by marrying and having scandalous affairs with women. OK, well, that doesn't sound like me, except for being attracted to men. But here are two comments from Leonid Sabaneeff, a close friend and biographer of Scriabin, that convinced me. First, Scriabin said of his effeminacy: "It's in us all, but I could not have

become what I am without *fostering* the masculine side and suppressing the feminine." And then, this amazing scene as Sabaneeff describes it:

> I almost never saw him "drunk," only high-spirited. He was very strong with regards to drink. Once in the summer of 1912, we were talking late and repaired to the Ampir Restaurant at the Petrovsky Railway Station . . . Scriabin, Podgeatsky, Dr. Bogorodsky, Baltrushaitis and I. We were there a long time and drank a lot. Scriabin was tipsy. When the waiters had blown out the candles, he took me by the hand and led me unsteadily through the darkened restaurant. He began kissing a few of the male guests still sitting around at tables alone, and introduced himself as a count, and me with some absurd double-barreled name. In his "languorous" voice he said, "The hour has come for us to know all about each other."

I can hear Paul breathing in the other room. Occasionally he turns, the bed creaks, he murmurs. I should be there with him. I should be joined with him in sleep, but my head, my head, my mind, my brain won't stop. My hand moves across the page as if possessed by some spirit. If I get it all on paper, I will sleep. I have to force it out of my head and keep it here. I want to sleep. I want to sleep. The sun is rising. The room, outside the area illuminated by my light, is growing a fuzzy gray. What is there to do but shower, dress, and begin the automaton dreariness of another day.

After Class

Angry. Depressed. Have to get through this. Have to persevere. Work was horrible. Arrived still buzzing from lack of sleep and by one I feigned illness and went home. Must have looked terrible because Barbara believed me. At home, slept until dusk and woke up disoriented, thirsty, and late for class. Ran to the music building on campus and found the group piano classroom, entering it just as the instructor was calling roll. She had only reached M but paused and looked up at me as I crept to an empty seat. I had never seen a classroom like this before. It consisted of four rows, each with four keyboards, and the instructor's desk, which also had a keyboard. Each student had a headset connected to the keyboard and several switches. Tentatively, I pressed one of the keys. Nothing happened. I pressed it a little harder. Still no sound. "Michael Van Allen," the instructor called, startling me. I responded. She was about forty, I would guess, very thin and wrinkled around her eyes. On the blackboard (green of course) was her name, written just like a prissy, perfect seventh grade girl would write it: Emma Richardson. "Van Allen," she repeated. I tensed. "You aren't related to Douglas Van Allen, are you?" Her tone was playful, as if this were a slightly ridiculous thought. "No," I replied. She smiled. "Lesson Number One, class. To play the piano well, you must listen to excellent pianists. Douglas Van Allen is one of the best playing today." She stood up and wrote Dad's name on the board in her girlish handwriting. "His recording of the Chopin études in particular." I hated her. Hated her bony hands, her tight little mouth, her cold, nasty eyes that sat behind her big glasses. "Now, class, everyone sit up straight and no one touch the keyboard yet. I want everyone to get used to the correct seating position. First, let's be sure you're the proper distance from the keyboard. Let the length of your fore-arm be your guide. Hands and arms should be relaxed . . ." On and on she droned, explaining how the class would work, how our keyboards worked. We all put on our headphones when instructed and flicked a switch. A little red light came on indicating the keyboard was working. You could then play and hear the notes. Emma had a control panel on her keyboard that would allow her to listen in on any student at any time, though there was no way for the student to know exactly when she was eavesdropping. She could also speak into a microphone and be heard by everyone. When she did this, we were all to stop playing immediately. Before we could practice, she went through all the basics—where middle C was, sharps and flats, correct finger positioning—all of which was review for me. Then she had us run through scales without our headphones as she walked around the room, correcting our fingers and posture. I found myself drawn to a dark-haired young man two rows in front of me who approached the silent scales with such seriousness. He had a little mole on his left cheek and a graceful, strong neck that reminded me of Paul. "Headphones on, everyone." Then things got bad. I was cocky, I guess. I figure I'd done this before. My scales were clumsy. This was so basic, and when I was eight years old I was able to do this in my sleep, but my fingers acted as if they had never been near a keyboard. I tried to concentrate and managed to do several perfect exam-ples before the fingers on one hand would tangle. There was no way to know when that hateful Emma was listening in. Occasionally, I swore I heard a faint click, but couldn't be sure if she was tuning in to my keyboard or tuning out. Whenever I looked up at her, she seemed to be looking my way and I would fumble again. By the end of the class, my nerves were shot. "Now, practice," Emma said in a singsong voice. "Practice, practice, practice. Every day without fail." When class was dismissed, I ran out of the room and charged home—alternately in fury and deep doubt. It was her ri-diculous approach that was causing my problems. No, I was too old. My fin-gers just wouldn't work the same way anymore. I was the oldest person in the class. It was degrading and ludicrous. If I had a different teacher, maybe a handsome male . . . if I had private lessons . . . if . . . if . . . if . . . By the time I got back to the apartment, I'd talked myself down a bit. I'd prac-tice and wouldn't let that horrible woman get in my way. It was all about doing it over and over again until you got it in your fingers. Until your fingers did the playing, not your brain. It had been years and it would be more difficult than I thought, but I had it in me. It's genetic. Look at Scriabin—his mother was a famous pianist. I presented a cheerful facade to Paul, telling him it went well, that it was like riding a bicycle. And for a while I believed it. I couldn't practice tonight, not with Paul home. I'll only be able to practice on the nights he's giving lessons or is at class. I can't handle knowing he's listening. I'm in the bedroom now as he works on the third movement of Samuel Barber's Piano Sonata—the centerpiece of his recital. I love to hear him play and the Barber is a beautiful, thorny piece. The third movement is a somber Adagio, the only slow, thoughtful part of the sonata. My favorite movement is the final one, a wild, thundering fugue, and given my mood I'd prefer he'd practice that part now. Each time he repeats a section, I listen for differences, trying to hear what displeased him or caused him a problem. Yet all I hear is beautiful music. Paul makes no errors that I can discern, so it's all technique and subtlety, which I fear will always elude me. It's why, as Madame Picone said after a year of her best efforts, I was a great music appreciator but a poor musician. She was trying to help, I suppose, but how do you say that to a ten-year-old and not wound? Imperious, frightening, enormous Madame Picone. How she would make me cower and yet, despite everything, why do I remember her fondly? Because I exasperated and confounded her and quite likely drove her to retirement? "A windup toy!" she shouted at me once in the middle of a lesson. "I can hear that you've practiced, but if I turn the crank it will sound the same next time. Where is the feeling?" Only when she shouted would any color come to her clown white face, a pale rose appearing everywhere simultaneously, from her double chin to her forehead where her hair was pulled so tightly into a bun that I thought her scalp might peel back like a tin can and reveal her pink, throbbing brain. That was the time I threw a temper tantrum, slammed down the keyboard cover, called her a stupid witch, ran out the door, and then had to wait on the dark street for half an hour before Mother came to pick me up. The next day, Madame Picone talked to Dad and told him I was a disturbed and unmusical child. He managed to convince her to keep me as a student until the group recital, after which they could reassess my musical future. Recital. "The frown." Hand injury. The end. Paul plays and plays. What must it be like to forget about the notes and have the music come out of you? Is it like channeling some spirit? No, Paul tells me, it's more like driving a car. The hand-eye coordination is second nature and the rest is concentration. Only sometimes, when you're in front of an audience and things are going really well and the adrenaline is pumping, does it seem like something else is happening. When I ask him to explain, he can only shrug. He's still in control, he says, so it's not like a waking dream or any romantic thing like that, but there's a release and a wonder when he's done. He's dazed, exhausted, and very, very happy. "Maybe it's different for other musicians," he tells me. "How does your Dad describe it?" Dad never talks about it. He thinks too much talk, too much discussion ruins the music. But I know he's a different man when he's on stage. And I know that the first time I saw him perform, I wanted to be just like him and experience what he experiences.

Much better now. Calm. Optimistic. A bit dreamy even. Tonight, I think, I'll have no trouble falling asleep.

How Sasha and I Are Alike

Sasha	Me
Injured his hand by overpracticing	Injured my hand by overpracticing
Feuded with his music instructors	Feuded with my music instructors
Was picked on as a young boy by the older cadets	Was taunted and beat up by jocks
Mother was a concert pianist	Father is a concert pianist
First wife was a concert pianist	Paul (second husband) is pianist
Hated Wagner's and Schubert's music	Think Schubert is boring
First marriage ended in divorce	Gerald dumped me
Frequently without money	Live from paycheck to paycheck
Father was frequently away	Dad tours for eight months each year
First large works were denigrated	First (and only) novel rejected
Suffered from insomnia	King of insomnia

How Sasha and I Are Different

Sasha	Me
Only child	Youngest child
Musical prodigy	Musical incompetent
Knew what he wanted to do from early age	Hardly
Haughty, self-assured	Frustrated, self-conscious
Frail and "ethereal"	Rarely catches cold
Mother died when he was very young	She's still here

Sasha Was Sexually Attracted to Men: More Evidence

Early influences: At age thirteen, Sasha was put under the tutelage of the famous and infamous Nikolai Zverev. This would virtually guarantee acceptance into the Moscow Conservatory. Zverev was the darling of Moscow high society, teaching royalty and the upper echelon in their homes and running a boarding school for aspiring young male pianists. He was also a notorious homosexual who, society gossips said, seduced many of his pensionnaires. Sasha was not a boarder and would arrive every Sunday for lessons. Zverev was amazed by little Sasha's ability to play by ear and to memorize large assignments effortlessly. Sasha became Zverev's favorite.

First crush: At age ten, Sasha made it clear he wished to enter the Cadet Corps—a military school with high academic standards where three of his uncles had attended, including his beloved Uncle Mitya. But all does not go well for Sasha at the corps. He is cruelly picked on and every attempt to show the older cadets how clever he was is met with scorn and name calling. He was regularly kicked and punched and subjected to merciless hazing. The cadets' ideal young man was strong and powerful, and in Sasha's first year, the most handsome, athletic, and powerful student was named Grisha. Sasha idolized him, even though Grisha joined in every time Sasha was tormented, and would watch Grisha practicing gymnastics, entranced. When Grisha performed his signature aerial somersault, Sasha would break into high-pitched, hysterical laughter. He gave Grisha his ration of milk. Did he want to be like Grisha? I don't think so. He just adored him.

Other evidence: "It is remarkable how there was invariably a male pattern laced with his contacts with women. Whenever he loved, there was a brother, husband, or son close at hand. His deepest attachments were with huge, massive, gruff men, totally contrasting from himself. All his six known heterosexual affairs were marked with undue publicity and scandal, as if to advertise himself . . . and counterbalance" (Faubion Bowers, *Scriabin: A Biography,* Dover Publications, 1996).

Sasha was prudish about sex in his conversations, unwilling to talk about it even in male company. He was never heard to utter any coarse or vulgar language. But his music is openly erotic. His notebooks are filled with sexual imagery only slightly obscured by his philosophical musings. I think he was sexually repressed and obsessed. If he were alive today, he'd be able to express all of that openly and become a sexual guru of sorts, an avant-garde artist combining music and performance and sex and cinema. He'd be banned and worshipped. He'd be the pansexual media god for the new century.

XxXxXx

Amazing, vivid dream that I have to write down before it fades.

For the second night in a row, I'd slept soundly. No insomnia. Tonight, we went to bed as usual around eleven and Paul was asleep in seconds, while I lay for a moment listening to his breathing. I had the sensation of floating you get just before you fall asleep. I remember thinking of water—a still pond with an enormous water lily blossoming on its surface. Then I woke up, or so I thought. It was still dark and I heard music coming from the living room, very soft, as if we'd left the CD player on and the volume turned low. Everything seemed normal at first, but suddenly there was a presence in the room, someone besides Paul. I tried to turn and look to see if Paul were still there, but I was frozen and only able to look up at the ceiling, which had a green phosphorescence like some glow-in-the-dark toy. Then I heard a man's voice say, "Get up." I rose out of bed and looked at Paul, who seemed to be just a pile of crumpled sheets. "Arise," the voice said and I did, floating up toward the glowing ceiling, which turned into an enormous face. It was Sasha. "Michael," he said. He spoke to me, offering encouragement in my plight, all the while the colors in his face changing and dancing, not like spotlights, but alive and pulsating. He continued speaking, but his face became an ocean and I was flying above it. I could distinguish each drop of water in the ocean and each drop of water was a different and distinct color, yet together they formed one blue-green sea. I could see both the specific drops and the whole of the ocean simultaneously. And in each drop and on the face of the entire sea, Sasha appeared, his eyes penetrating and compassionate. He kept talking and I tried to remember the words, but they seemed to evaporate as I heard them, leaving nothing. Then a sun rose from the sea and though it was bright, I could look directly into it. At its center was a staring, androgynous face, its eyes outlined in heavy black, its nose like a thick, downward-pointing arrow, its mouth a straight line. It stared at me as though I were an insect it wanted to squash. Then the sea began to rise up to me in a column of color and light, licking and fluttering over me like a tongue. I heard Sasha crying out, "Oh, what is coming! What is coming! You are on the road to Ecstasy!" I grew excited, erect, as the water ebbed and flowed over me and just as I was ready to climax, I woke up.

And this is the part I can't explain.

I wasn't in bed. I was sitting at the kitchen table, naked, with a burning hard-on. I had a pen in my hand and on a paper towel I had written in a weird, spidery scrawl every word I'd heard Sasha say in the dream. I just sat there for a long time, my heart racing, terribly, terribly frightened. Then I read the words on the paper towel again, which I've copied here:

Love life with all your being, and you will be happy forever. Never fear to be what you wish to be. Never fear your desires. Grow sumptuous. Develop all your talents. Study my laws of time and space and follow them exactly. *Look upon each unpleasantness only as an obstacle, as a sign* that you have the *powers to defeat it.* If you fret and regret that you have no *talent,* then this is a sign that the seed of *talent* is in you. Let it grow and never doubt it. I wish to awaken in your consciousness a desire for insane, unlimited bliss. You are intoxicated by my fragrance, awakened by my kiss licking you and fluttering over you. You are made languid and feminine by the sweet tenderness of my proximity, are quickened by the lightning flashes of my passion. You will feel the glorious birthing of your dreams.

I recognize the words, could hear his voice passionately intoning them. I must burn the paper towel before Paul wakes up. I can't have him finding it. It is a message to me and me alone.

XxXxXx

seed of talent

XxXxXx

I never know where Dad is and when he's available, so it's not practical to just call him up. I have to go through Mother, who has the numbers and schedules. She then tells me when the best times to call are and makes me commit to one of them. This is why I rarely call him—it's such a production. Mother was so happy to find out I wanted to talk to him, though, and was even happier when I told her I'd be coming to Dad's recital. Mother insists that everything be neat and tidy. I think it's because painting is so messy. Everything else in her life needs to be under her control. That's why she is so meticulous about Dad's schedule and why it bothers her that I've turned out to be the one member of the family she has trouble keeping tabs on. Karl and Sara live within twenty minutes of Mother and Dad. The whole family, minus me, has dinner together whenever Dad gets back to town. I'm the proverbial black sheep in so many ways—from shit job to nonstandard domestic arrangement—so when I actually do what she wants me to do, her exuberance is particularly annoying. I try to imagine what it's like to be her and to let go of my irritation. She's getting older. She wants to know that all of her children are happy and will gather around her in times of need. Occasions such as the recital and her opening are just dress rehearsals for the later, more catastrophic events she's sure to face. Well, she's got Karl and Sara. They'll be there. Why should I have to be involved? Amy can take my place so that Mother won't feel she's lost a child. Reading back over this, I realize I sound cruel. It's difficult to explain how oppressive my family is—the expectations, disappointments, pity, and disgust I can see in their eyes when they look at me. I went to a therapist for years to try to deal with all this—as if it was my fault that they feel this way about me—and all I got out of the experience was a stronger conviction that my family saw me as someone to be pitied. Thanks, Dr. Jamison. What would I have ever done without you? So Mother was thrilled that I was "coming home" and I'm sure she got in touch with Dad to let him know when I'd be calling. What a happy, spontaneous family I have. I wanted to talk to Dad about playing Scriabin. My second piano class was even more frustrating than the first. I was in need of—well, certainly not encouragement, for I didn't even want Dad to know I was taking piano lessons again. I was in need of perspective. I wanted to find out what's waiting for me on the other side of this purgatory of scales and exercises, what would it be like to play this music that cast its spell on me. In the past three days, I've probably listened to the CD twenty times—mostly at night, wearing headphones, when I was supposed to be asleep. I don't need to sleep much. I'm functioning pretty well at work, though I do call in sick from time to time—like yesterday—not because I'm tired but because I hate my job. Just knowing that I won't be at work relaxes me so much that I fall asleep for most of the day. I don't think my boss believes me anymore, though, when I call in sick. And Paul caught me in a lie about that as well, which led to our fight. And despite not sleeping, I've managed to practice for piano class, not that it's made much of a difference since knowing Evil Emma might be listening in on me makes all my practice abandon me. I stayed home from work yesterday. Tuesday is a good day to call in sick, first because calling in sick on a Monday or Friday is too obvious, and second because Paul has class and gives lessons, so he's on campus all day and never gets home before I do. Almost never. Except for yesterday. He got home early and found me asleep on the sofa, so he woke me up and wanted to know why I wasn't at work. I could have just said I was sick or that I needed sleep, but then Paul would want me to go to a doctor. He thinks my insomnia is getting worse and that I need help. I just can't explain to him that I'm wired differently. I'm a night owl and don't need to sleep every night. But I'm forced into this nine-to-five thing. So I told him I'm sick of my job and that some days I just can't face it. That's what sick days are for, really. I rarely get sick. Then Paul starts saying I'm stubborn and immature and reminds me that we need two paychecks to pay the rent and to buy groceries and I start getting defensive and accuse Paul of not understanding what it's like to work at a shitty job that you hate. He's always done what he loves. People like that really can't understand. "Then find a job you do like," Paul shouts. "Preferably one that pays better." Whenever Paul raises his voice, I start crying. It's just this automatic reaction, like closing your eyes when you see a strong light. Paul held me for a while, though I could tell he was still pissed off. There was a stiffness to his body, an unwillingness to give me everything I needed. That got me desperate, so I started to kiss him. We haven't had sex very often lately and Paul responded. As we kissed, I wondered if Paul was more attracted to the idea that my father was Douglas Van Allen than he was attracted to me. I had to pull away and tell Paul I was too tired to continue. He was pissed off. "Why did you start it then? What is with you? Does this give you a weird thrill or something?" I told him I was just tired and that he was making a big deal out of nothing. "You're acting like a dog in heat," I said. For a second I thought he was going to slap me. Instead, he spoke very softly and turned away. "I don't like you very much right now." I couldn't help myself. I said "I don't think you like me at all. You just like my last name." "Oh, shut up, Mike," Paul said. His tone was flat. He seemed bored. "Just sleep it off and let's both forget you said anything that insulting and pathetic. I'll wake you when dinner's ready." I went into the bedroom and collapsed. I had no trouble falling asleep. When Paul woke me, we ate, though we didn't talk much. I felt like crap. Today, though, I managed to drag myself to work.

My window of opportunity to call Dad was between 7:00 and 7:30 this evening. He'd be in his hotel suite in Cleveland. His assistant Jen answered the phone. I'd never met her, but Mother said she was no-nonsense, about thirty-five, pale, and "not very attractive." I'm sure Mother had a hand in hiring her. Jen was protective of Dad's privacy, so getting past her must have been difficult for most people. Since I knew her name, was on "the family list," and was expected to call around this time, I got Dad on the line in seconds. First we did the chitchat thing. It's so wonderful that I'm coming to the recital and Mother's opening. How's Cleveland? (A nice city despite all those rumors to the contrary.) How's piano class going? (It figures Mother would have to tell him about that.) I changed the subject and told him I'd been reading a lot about Scriabin as well as listening to his piano music. "Oh?" Dad asked. "Which recording?" I started to say Horowitz, then caught myself, quickly changing the *Ho* into an *Oh*. "Oh, your CD, of course," I lied. "And another one with some sonatas on it. Horowitz, I think." "He's the master," Dad said, "but he's hardly the last word on Scriabin." I launched into my questions. I was trying to get him to tell me what it was like to play Scriabin and to find out whether he's read any of the philosophy. But getting Dad to talk to me about music was a chore. He won't discuss technique because I'm not a fellow pianist and I wouldn't understand anyway. So he'd try to come up with layperson's descriptions that were too simplistic for me. "And the philosophy," Dad said, putting the word *philosophy* in quotation marks, "well, I don't see the point of any of it. His music is what matters." I asked if knowing what Scriabin had in his head, what the ideas were behind the music, would help Dad play. Look at the "Poem of Ecstasy." Scriabin wrote an entire poem as a prelude to writing the symphonic work and the Fifth Sonata. It had to have some significance. "I feel like I'm talking to some damn music critic," Dad said. He was trying to sound jovial, but he was annoyed as well. "Scriabin wanted people to listen to the music. If he needed to write a poem to help his music come out, that's fine, but it has nothing to do with the actual music. If it did, the music wouldn't be worth playing." I asked him if he'd read the poem. "No," he replied, as though the thought were absurd. "I looked at it. Michael, Scriabin ended up going insane. The poem is the scribbling of a deluded egomaniac who also happened to be a musical genius. As with many geniuses, though, his insanity seemed to help him create beautiful, amazing works. It's the music that's important. The rest is insignificant background noise. Why are you so interested in this?" I told him I was reading a biography and started to wonder about it. "Well, that's great, Michael," he said. "You know I'm always happy when you take an interest in things, but I just hope you can hear the music without filtering it through all that nonsense about Spirit and Ecstasy and whatever other words Scriabin chose to turn into proper nouns." "Maybe he wasn't insane," I said. "Some of it makes sense." "You think so?" Dad asked. "Well, you better keep that to yourself or we'll have to take you to see Dr. Jamison before you start thinking you're God." Why did he have to say that? Why does he always have to be right and I always have to be wrong? Then I told him that I was thinking about trying to play some Scriabin. "There aren't many of his pieces suitable for the casual player," he said. "Maybe the early ones." I couldn't help getting angry, though I just sounded whiny. I told him that this wasn't just a hobby. I wanted to learn to play well. "Of course, Michael," he said, and he couldn't help sounding patronizing. "Never take up anything unless you want to do it well. I'd recommend, though, that you start out more traditionally. Set your sights on obtainable goals." I knew I had to hang up before he started asking me about the paralegal studies program that I had no intention of ever enrolling in. After the call, I started to feel sorry for Dad. I realized he'd probably never be able to perform Scriabin very well because he was simply playing the notes. Sasha had spoken to me and said, "Study my laws of time and space and follow them exactly." The name Van Allen will eventually be linked to Scriabin, just as the name Horowitz is, but it won't be Douglas Van Allen. I just have to believe and overcome the obstacles. Sasha will help. His Spirit has chosen me. It sounds ridiculous. It sounds crazy, but it's the truth. Sasha's music has awakened in me a joy I'd never imagined before. Poor Dad. He'll never understand.

The seed of talent is in me.

I'm on the verge of discovering a monumental truth. Paul is so busy practicing for his recital next week that I've had a lot of time to myself. I've been studying Sasha's "Poem of Ecstasy." I haven't listened to the symphonic *Poem of Ecstasy* yet. I have to understand the poem first. But I'm getting closer, and in preparation I stole a CD containing the *Poem of Ecstasy* and *Prometheus: Poem of Fire,* Sasha's last completed work. "Stole" sounds so criminal, but I didn't feel guilty. I was meant to have the CD. Before I can listen to it, I have to decipher the text. At first it didn't make much sense. It's long and rambling and I've never been much of a poetry reader, so I stumbled through it a few times and read some commentary, which gave a very simplistic explanation of a Creator, a Man-God, who is identified as Sasha and who gives to us, gives to the world, Ecstasy and liberation. But I couldn't shake the sense that there was another message hidden in the poem, maybe a message that couldn't be understood by reading the poem in a traditional way. What if the poem was a code?

OoOoOoOoOoOoOoOoOoOoOoOoOoOoOoOoOoOo

Spirit Winged Is On There Emerges Of Spirit Spirit Spirit, Winged life is flight On negation There emerges feeling Spirit desiring Spirit Surrenders Mid It From Calls And It dream love creations languor inspiration flower soaring oblivion Desiring Spirit, playing Spirit Feelings and forms heavenly of world magical emerges, dream its of rays the under, there Negation of summits the on flight into drawn is, life for thirst with Winged, Spirit

OoOoOoOoOoOoOoOoOoOoOoOoOoOoOoOoOoOo

I've filled up scraps of paper with different combinations of words, arranging the letters so they line up, then studying them for secret acrostic meanings. Though I've found nothing conclusive yet, it's mysteriously calming, replacing sleep for me. In the morning, I'm fresh, clearheaded. I'm able to go about my day disguised as a normal human being and no one suspects the work I'm doing, the real work, not the ridiculous work that brings in money. The secret of the poem is not a secret that can be written down and understood. Yet I try. With persistence and belief, I try.

OoOoOoOoOoOoOoOoOoOoOoOoOoOoOoOoOoOo

intense red orange yellow green sky blue pearly blue bright blue violet purple lilac flesh rose deep red human will creative play joy matter dreams contemplation creativity will of the creative spirit will of the creative spirit movement of spirit into matter humanity lust diversification of will intense red orange yellow green moonshine pearly blue bright blue violet purple lilac glint of steel steel deep red human will creative play joy matter dreams contemplation creativity will of the creative spirit will of the creative spirit movement of spirit into matter humanity passion diversification of will intense red orange yellow green frost pearly blue bright blue violet purple lilac flesh rose deep red

OoOoOoOoOoOoOoOoOoOoOoOoOoOoOoOoOoOo

Paul oppresses me. I went to his recital, but the music meant nothing. I can't believe I once found any of it beautiful. Paul is always talking about jobs and everyday commitments. He seems to have labeled each day— Garbage Day, Laundry Day, Grocery Day. It bores me and keeps me from my work on the poem. I've given up the piano lessons as well. They teach me nothing and I'm beginning to believe that rote memorization and practicing are harmful to the music. Playing Scriabin is not about practicing. What a ludicrous thought! What a Douglas Van Allen thought! I shuffle to the law firm every day, but I can't concentrate on the details anymore. I go home sick sometimes because I am sick of it all. I'm trading my time for a paycheck, which allows me to live. Biding my time. I have to make them all believe I'm a good worker, a good soldier, a good boy, a good good good boy for just a while longer. The poem continues to elude me, but I never tire of it as I do of everything else. I have to hide this notebook every night. I can't have Paul discovering that I've changed. Not yet. I have to keep up my front. I'm a spy, watching everything happen. I'm smiling and talking about TV shows and grocery shopping. I'm undercover in this world, in this reality. Once I thought that I cared for people and cared about what they thought of me. I don't care. I thought I loved Paul. I don't. What I called love wasn't even an emotion. What I called Love is a Word, a Husk, a Dead Thing. What I called Love stands for something that doesn't even exist in the reality we call our day-to-day world. Eventually, I'll be able to cast it away. I'll be able to split out of my cocoon and understand that life was just the shadows cast by the glorious other world as the light from an unseen sun, the real Sun, played across the inside of my cocoon. We're all in co-coons. Douglas, Marta, Sara, Karl, Amy, Paul, Dr. Jamison, Evil Emma, Madame Picone are all dead husks living in dead cocoons. Michael is pushing against his cocoon. Waiting for the crack to widen. Waiting.

OoOoOoOoOoOoOoOoOoOoOoOoOoOoOoOoOo

Spirit Is There. Winged life is flight. On negation there emerges feeling. Spirit, desiring Spirit, surrenders. It dreams love, creations, languor, inspi-ration. Flower soaring. Oblivion. Desiring Spirit, playing Spirit, feelings and forms heavenly, magical, emerge. Dreams of rays. The under. There. Ne-gation of summits. Flight into drawn. Life for thirst. Thirst for life. Winged Spirit.

OoOoOoOoOoOoOoOoOoOoOoOoOoOoOoOoOo

Had to get away from Paul. I had to just leave—in the middle of another ar-gument about the way I'm acting. Acting. I'm not acting anymore. Paul and everyone like him are the actors. I've seen what's outside. Paul just looks at me like I'm the crazy one. He just looks at me. Can't even speak. I wish he was overcome by the truths I've learned, but I can't tell him everything.

What I can tell him makes him just look at me. So I leave, right in the middle of it all. I leave with no idea where I'm going, wander off into the night without a word. There's nothing to say. I'm not yet beyond words, though. I write words. I speak words to fit in. My Time has not yet come, though it is closer and closer each day. Sasha has given me another sign. He has appeared to me—not in a dream. He has appeared to me—not in a vision. There was a manifestation. His Spirit, the Spirit, appeared and gave me a sign. I was wavering and he gave me a sign so I would know my Time of Ecstasy was coming. I was wavering. I left Paul in the middle of the argument, except it was no argument because he just looked at me. I walked and walked in the night and came to rest on a bench under a tree. It was a park. I'd been in the park before, but it was night and deserted and seemed a different place. I sat on the park bench and looked at the night and the stars and the shadows and heard the sounds of the park at night—the crickets and the hum beneath night silence. The hum beneath everything. The hum that, if you listen long enough and close enough, becomes music. I listened to the night hum turn into sad, unorganized chords. I sat in the park and looked at the stars and I regretted walking out on Paul. I wanted him to come with me on my journey. I'd miss him. I wondered if I'd done the right thing, wondered if my sacrifices would be worth it. So I left the park and the night hum and found my way back to the apartment. Paul was gone. When he returned, I told myself, I would try to make things right. I'd go undercover a bit longer, be a good boy, until the Time was at hand. Then Sasha appeared, seated at the piano. He turned to face me. With a nod, he reaffirmed that everything was going as it should. He sat with his hands resting on his knees and I was startled by the sound of music coming from the piano. Sasha nodded again and the music stopped. His lips didn't move, but his voice said, "Push the music out and it will manifest." I did. I thought of a note—C. I focused on the note, then pushed it out. From the piano, I heard middle C being played. The key did not depress, but the note was loud. Sasha's hands had not moved. "The seed of talent is in you," I heard his voice say. "Never doubt it." Then he was gone.

It's now very late and Paul has still not come home. I'm exhausted from playing the piano. It takes a great deal of effort to make the notes sound without touching the keys. When Paul returns, I can't tell him about my new skill. It's not time yet. When Paul returns, we'll make love and talk of dead concerns, of cocoon emotions. When he returns, we'll talk and he won't just look at me. I'm no longer concentrating on the music, and the nighttime hum replaces the sound of the chords. I've brought the hum with me from the park. It seeps into my skin and dissolves in my blood like a gas, keeping me tranquil and cooled and immobile until the time when Paul returns.

OoOoOoOoOoOoOoOoOoOoOoOoOoOoOoOo

Spirit desiring oblivion. But again. From submerged Spirit, bright world. Spirit triumphant. Alas emptiness. But dreaming. But life. O beatitude, delighting Ecstasy in freedom. I, daring. Now me. When Play, O mine, with world new. And again. Then mysterious. Wave joy, you feelings, you desires, you unity. Bliss completely. Eternity affirmation. Ecstasy. Universe flames, being tides, power will menace. Seduction. Frightened pleasure. Hyena caresses sting, kiss, resound, cry, I am

part three

ecstasy

1

I watch the light change. The winter sun disappears behind the houses across the street. Color is draining from the apartment, but I don't want to turn on a lamp. I want everything to be fuzzy and gray, melting into shadows and vague shapes. I've come to the end. The other Michael wrote no more. An angle of streetlight shows me a chair, a picture on the wall, but the rest of the apartment is quiet and dark at last.

The clocks tick.

Paul will be home soon.

I hear the heater switch on, and then a rumbling joins the ticking clocks. I can acknowledge or ignore these household noises at will. Here. Gone. Here. Gone. It comforts me.

The other Michael is in the apartment as well. He hovers like the hum of the heater, like the cars passing on the street. He crouches here next to me in the shadows and whispers.

Here. Gone. Here.

I don't have to believe what he tells me. If I can't remember it, then it didn't happen like that.

"Something happened," the other Michael says.

"No," I tell him. "Nothing happened at all."

A key turns in the lock. The front door opens.

"Mike?" Paul says. I hear a click and the shadows are gone. I shield my eyes and look at him. He carries a large grocery bag. "Are you OK?"

The overhead light is too bright. Paul's face is bleached and gaunt and a little frightening.

"Hello," I say, but don't stand up. "I didn't realize it was so late." I don't remember moving from the piano bench to the floor.

Paper bags crumple. I can hear glass and tin and cardboard clunk and scrape against the countertop. It's too loud and I move my hands up to cover my ears, then stop. How could I explain that to Paul? The groceries are hurting my ears. I'm not crazy anymore. I have to keep from doing crazy things.

"I bought some broccoli and some shrimp. I thought we'd stir-fry tonight," he says, calling to me as if I was lost somewhere in the depths of the apartment.

"Stir-fry. Yes," I call back. I force the kitchen sounds to recede. They join the clocks and the heater and the shadows. The other Michael is gone.

"What did you do today?" Paul asks. "I hope you stayed in. It was cold and wet."

"Mozart," I say. "I listened to Mozart."

"That's all?" He's come into the living room. "A whole day of Mozart." His tone is cheerful and forced. "You should be very relaxed."

"I read, too." The words come out quickly.

"Oh?" Paul says, interested. "That's good." He leans down to kiss me, then strokes my hair and goes into the kitchen.

"What did you read?"

I'm holding my breath as I glance around the room.

Paul says very casually, "Can you remember?"

"Yes." The kitchen noises are louder again, emerging from the background as though someone had turned up the volume on a radio.

"I'm just curious, Mike. Tell me what you read."

"Some silly things. Magazines." I have to shout to be heard over the crashing of the paper bags and the grating of metal.

Paul is standing in the doorway to the kitchen, looking at me. Only then do I realize my hands are over my ears. I try to make it look as though I'm only scratching, but Paul's face tells me he's not fooled.

"What's the matter?" The wonder and fear in his voice breaks inside me. I inhale one ragged breath that bursts out in three short sobs. The feeling is old, familiar, beyond comfort or pain. Paul's arms are around me. He nestles my head into his chest.

Then it's gone. We're still. I don't want to move away from Paul.

"Magazines," I say at last, my voice just a whisper. "I read some magazines."

"It's OK." He kisses the side of my face. "It's OK."

"I'm fine. I'm not crazy anymore."

Paul is quiet for a very long time, then he says, "I talked to a doctor today."

His words make my body tighten, compacting from the center outward. I try to move away from him, but Paul's arms tense with me and won't let go.

"Listen to me for a minute," Paul says. "I worry about you, Mike. I want what's best for you. You're here by yourself all day. You don't talk to anyone. It's not good."

"I was reading magazines. I listened to Mozart." My voice is growing smaller and my body is shrinking as well.

"The doctor is someone for you to talk to. That's all. He's a friend of Kevin and Joe. I told him all about you. He thinks he can help."

I have no idea who Kevin and Joe are, and I begin to suspect I don't really know who Paul is either.

"Think about it," he says. "Promise me you'll think about calling him?"

I nod.

"Are you feeling better? Let's have some dinner, OK? Maybe we can go to a movie later. Do you want to go out?" He releases me from his grip and stands up. "Why don't you sit on the sofa?" He offers me his hand and I take it. "Or you can help me in the kitchen. Cut up the broccoli? Peel the shrimp?"

I just want Paul to stop talking. "Can we stay in tonight?" I ask. "I'm still tired."

He bites his lip. "It would do you good to get out. Be around people."

I shake my head. "No. Not tonight."

He's still holding my hand. Behind him, in the shadows just beyond the bedroom's doorway, I see the other Michael. He's looking at me, then steps backward into the darkness and is gone. I let go of Paul's hand.

"Can I just listen to some music?" I ask. "Maybe some piano music?"

Paul looks a bit disappointed. My feelings for him have drained away, like colors at dusk.

A blanket covers me. It's dark. The clock on the table glows. It says 3:22. My head is clear and empty.

I sit up. Beside me is a man with long hair that spreads out across the pillow. He has thrown the blanket off and is naked. I watch his breathing. I've never seen him before.

Where am I? What's my name?

I breathe—rapidly at first, then slower, slower. Taking the air in, filling my lungs, pushing the panic out. Slowly, slowly. The fear subsides, leaving behind the apartment, the bedroom, my name, and Paul.

In a corner of the room, the other Michael watches me from the protective darkness. I can hear him whispering.

"Oh what is coming! What is coming!"

In the daylight, my situation seems less dire, though for the first time, I'm nervous about being alone all day. The sky hasn't cleared, but the rain has stopped, at least for the morning. I try to think of things to do. Perhaps I will go to the grocery store or meet Paul for lunch. Paul has no commitments until ten, so there is no hurry to get out of bed. It's just as well. After waking up earlier, I slept very little.

Paul's body is warm. His arms wrap around me and I clutch them to my chest and press closer. I think, like me, he is half-awake and yet still dreaming. My thoughts move and melt between my daytime concerns and images that might be memories or might be dreams, brought on and enhanced, it seems, by my reading the journal, which I returned to its hiding place before we went to bed. Perhaps sleeping on top of it is causing a kind of transference. There are strange and wonderful patterns of color and I can see myself walking past and through them as if they were pictures in a museum or enormous soap bubbles. Behind me must be the sun, for my back is warm, then I return to the bed and know it is Paul, not the sun, and I'm awake again.

He shifts, pulls me closer, kisses the curve of my neck. The backs of my thighs begin to burn as his penis pushes against them. Yesterday I responded eagerly, but this morning it seems to ruin the blissful comfort and warmth we're sharing. I keep my thighs tense and hope his passion will go away, ebb to a soft heat and allow me to dream again. Instead, Paul becomes more insistent. He pushes. His hands move across my chest and his tongue flicks along my back and neck. He is awake now. I stay still and pretend I'm asleep. My thighs remain together. Again he pushes, then moves his hand down to my penis, which is soft and shriveled as if in disgust. I pretend to wake up, and he rolls me onto my back, kissing me deeply. I don't kiss him back. There's no excitement, no heat. He moves his weight onto me. I can't breathe.

"No," I say as his hands move down my sides.

He stops and rolls off me, embarrassed.

"OK," he says flatly.

I realize that now I have an erection and the tone in Paul's voice seems too final. Inexplicably the sight of Paul—confused and limp— arouses me more. The warmth of the bed caresses me.

"Wait," I say, "come here." My voice is low.

Paul's face goes blank, then his eyes narrow. He stands up.

"Jesus Christ," he says, sounding very tired. "Here we go again. I thought you'd changed." His voice is quiet, but his eyes are shouting at me.

I have done something wrong, I think. I can't speak. I can only look at Paul, my mouth open.

"No. Yes. Hot. Cold. I can't go through this again. I won't." He moves around the room, jamming his legs into jeans, fumbling with buttons on a shirt. "Did you know I started seeing a therapist? I thought all this was my fault. Maybe I was the one with the problems. But it's you. It's always been you, hasn't it?"

Paul leaves and I can hear him in the bathroom. All I can do is pull the blanket around me to hide my nakedness. He comes back, fully dressed, holding a hairbrush.

"I have to go earn some money," he says. "The doctor's name and number are on the kitchen table. Find time in your busy schedule to call and make an appointment."

He stares at me, waiting.

There's nothing I can say that would make any sense. There's no excuse, no apology that would be sincere.

Paul turns and walks out. I hear him put on his coat and gather up his scores. Then he's gone.

The clocks tick. Upstairs, the little man stomps across the floor. I lay in bed for hours.

When I do get up, I take a long shower, cleaning up after myself, eating, doing the dishes—anything that keeps me from thinking or having to make a decision. I look at the doctor's name and telephone number. The card sits on the kitchen table, but I don't touch it. When my back is turned, I still know it's there. His name is Dr. Ken Hammond. When there's nothing more for me to do, I sit on the sofa in the living room and look out the window. The sun has come out. I can see students on their way to classes. They carry their coats. It looks warm. A light breeze blows their hair.

I won't be here when Paul returns. I can't be. The sun is shining. The rain has stopped.

I close my eyes and focus my thoughts. I push and send one thought into the sunlight. *Karl.*

In the phone book, I find a number for directory assistance. I tell the man which city, then spell Karl's name. A mechanical voice speaks the numbers separately with odd inflections. It takes me two attempts to write the number down.

Amy answers.

"Mike," she shouts, "are you all right? Are you with Paul?"

"I'm fine. Is Karl there?"

"He's at work, Mike. I can have him call you when he gets home tonight."

"Can I call him at work?" I ask, trying not to sound anxious. "Is that OK? I have to ask him something."

Amy hesitates. "He may be in court today," she says. "I'm not sure."

I push. *Karl.*

"OK," she says and gives me the number.

When he answers the telephone, his voice is so curt and business-like yet so familiar that I hang up. The sunlight gives the living room a warmth and brightness I haven't seen before, yet I'm at odds with it. People walk by on the street, some laughing and talking, some smiling or just thinking, and I wonder how they keep from feeling as I do—shut off, closed down.

The doctor's name and phone number are still written on a piece of paper which lies on the kitchen table. The sun is so warm, the sky so clear. I won't need a coat. There's nothing here I want to take with me—not even the photograph of Paul and me, looking happy. I guess I was happy once. Or the other Michael was. We're becoming more alike—the other Michael and I—and although that seems the point of my getting better and returning to this life I can't remember, I don't want what the other Michael offers. His memories are not comforting. Can't I start from here? Can't I be *this* Michael?

No, the sunlight seems to tell me. Not here, the clocks chant. Not in these places. These are the other Michael's places, his people, his dreams.

I won't need a coat. No umbrella. All I'll keep is some of the other Michael's clothes. I can't go naked. That would be crazy, and I'm not. That's the other Michael. I never was crazy. I'm new, come into existence just now, this morning, in this sunlight.

Most of the people on the street are walking in the same direction, so I start out going the other way. With each person who passes me, a piece of the other Michael disappears, as if he's a disintegrating cloak I wear. Squares of threadbare incidents and vague memories are caught by the wind and flutter away. The sunlight and the air purify me. I can feel it.

The streets are lined with shade trees, though they are bare of leaves and cast shadows of their branches on the sidewalk—twisting, elegant shapes that reach out to me, grab hold, then pull me along until the next tree and the next shadows. The houses are older, some with porches, but all of them looking deserted and damp from recent rains, their evergreen shrubbery so bright it glows. Ahead I see more green and more leafless trees and the road and sidewalk turn to go around them. It's a park with brown grass and a bench in the sun near the pines. A water fountain. No one else is about.

The sky in the distance is dark with clouds. The sunlight won't stay after all, but here in the park it's warm and if I sit on the bench and face away from the clouds, it's as if they're not there. It must be spring. There are birds fluttering about, calling to each other in the trees. I see buds everywhere, ready to burst. Under my feet, pine needles crunch, smelling wet and evergreen. The scent of roses mixes with the pine. My face is warm. My hands are warm. I take off my shoes and socks and bury my feet in the cool pine needles.

I've forgotten my name, but that doesn't matter. There is just me, whoever I am, and the park and the trees and the bench. The sunlight makes me sleepy. Perhaps I've been awake all night. Perhaps I live somewhere near here.

There's no one about.

I take off my shirt and roll it into a pillow for my head. I'll take a nap, here in the sun by the pine trees. Just a short nap. When I wake up, perhaps I'll remember who I am, where I am. I lay down on the bench, which doesn't feel like a bench anymore. It's soft and warm. I close my eyes and imagine I'm in bed. The sun is my blanket. I'm dreaming. I am.

2

"Get up," someone whispers. It's dark. I can't open my eyes or move. I hear water falling all around me. I'm cold. I'm damp.

"Get up." It's a man's voice. He speaks louder this time. Again I try to move, but it's as if I'm frozen, and I begin to shiver in the wetness.

"Arise!" The voice booms around me and inside me. With a snap, my eyes are open and I'm propelled upward so fast that all I can see are streaks of light, then my movement slows, and I can make out dark clouds. Rain is falling, yet I'm no longer cold or wet. I've stopped moving. In the park below me, a man is lying on the bench, without a shirt. He looks asleep or even dead. The sun is gone and the rain has returned, pouring down on the landscape. I can see streetlights and houses and people running under umbrellas that glisten. A woman hurries by the man on the bench and she slows, her umbrella turning as she looks, then continues on her way.

"Don't go," I shout, but the words exist only inside me. All I hear is wind and the rain hitting the ground. The man on the bench twitches.

"You are free," the voice says. I have no body. I am sight and thought. It is Sasha's voice, though transformed, seeming to come from all around me.

Above me, there is a break in the clouds and I'm engulfed in a flash of white heat. Then my vision slowly clears. I can hear birds calling, insects buzzing. The whiteness coalesces into areas of green and brown, shadows and sunlight, as I realize I'm in a wooded glade, surrounded by birch. I look down and see hands, a body. I smell trees. A bug flies into my ear.

"Come look!"

A young girl in a long white dress waves to me. She has black hair held back with a blue ribbon and she carries a basket.

"It's a perfect ring." She smiles and spreads her arms. I can see she is standing in the middle of a large mushroom circle. She laughs. The basket is full of red and brown and golden mushrooms.

"We shan't pick them. It's a fairy ring."

She sets down the basket and takes my hand. "Sasha," she says, her eyes lowered, then looks up at me. I can hear her thoughts. *Draw me near. Kiss me, darling.*

"Change it." Sasha's voice is everywhere, yet the girl seems to hear nothing. She waits for her kiss.

There is another flash of light.

"Alexander Nikolaievich!"

A handsome, broad-faced young man waves at me. His collarless shirt is open, revealing his throat and a hint of his chest. His sleeves are rolled. He carries the same basket.

"Come look! It's a perfect ring."

I walk toward him. His hair is black and falls over one side of his face. He pushes it back, then spreads his arms, raising the basket. I step into the circle of mushrooms and give him my hand. He smiles with just a hint of a smirk and sets the basket down.

"Shall we lie down for a bit?" he asks, his voice quiet. "It's a fairy ring." My heart pounds. He takes my hand and draws me near.

"Sasha," he whispers. "Shurinka." His breath smells of sunflower seeds. His eyes are deep blue.

We kiss, a hard kiss that travels through me like a shock. He tears at my shirt and we tumble to the ground in a swirl of butterflies. I can taste his tongue and smell the heat of his smooth, pale skin.

There is another flash. The forest is gone and I'm enveloped in a swirl of color and music. Sasha speaks, his voice welling out of the sound and light. Again, I am formless.

"Just a morsel," he says. "You can return to it when you like. I have more to show you."

His face appears, coalescing from the colors, enormous and strangely comforting.

"With mysterious delights of unknown feelings, with myriads of dream and vision," he intones, his eyes blazing green and violet, his mouth and beard pulsing pearly blue, then rose, his forehead glinting of steel and frost. "With inspiration's flame of Truth seeking, with the forbidden wish of divine freedom. O my beloved, I shall come. Your dream of me is being born. It is I."

Sasha's face and all the colors rush sideways in a blur. I'm spinning, gaining shape, growing heavy. When my vision clears, I am sitting at a piano in a dark room lit only by oil lamps. In front of me are sheets of music paper covered with frenzied scratchings. I hold a pencil in one small, frail-looking hand and continue adding notes to the score with amazing speed. My head is pounding. My eyes burn. I can hear music inside me, maddening music that repeats until I manage to move it onto the page. Then I throw the pencil down and begin to play what I've written. My hands know what to do. The notes on the page are as clear to me as words in a sentence, their meanings decipherable and complete.

Behind me, a door opens. "Shurinka," a woman says. "Darling, you must sleep." She stands beside me, a plain little woman with an oval face and thick, carefully plucked eyebrows that arch in perpetual amazement. Her dress is long and dark, her neck unseen in a high ruffled collar.

"Later, Auntie," I say. It's a young boy's voice. "It won't stop, this music in my head. I must write it down."

The room spins and I am still at the piano, though it elongates and transforms into a black and gleaming concert grand. My hands are larger, the fingers long and delicate. To my right is a row of bright lights and beyond them I hear many people murmuring, coughing. I wait, my hands resting on my knees, until they are quiet. Then, with a nod, I begin to play. My left hand pounds on the lower keys, growling, then with both hands I skip up the length of the keyboard. It's the Fifth Sonata. I'm playing it from memory, my hands caressing, then flying across the keys, the right foot stepping on the pedals as if it were possessed, the notes whirling in a vortex of sound. My body tenses, then expands, now soft, now hard, until the final notes seem to fly into the ether and ring for just an instant before the applause comes over the footlights.

Again everything spins. I'm in a small bed and over me are pained, worried faces. Some of the women are ringing their hands. All the men have large mustaches or beards. I recognize Aunt Lyubov, my wife Tatyana, my old friend Leonid Sabaneeff, Dr. Bogorodsky. I *know* these people. My upper lip is swollen and throbbing with pain. A sheet covers my face below my eyes and I am burning with fever. Leonid leans closer to me.

"What a scandal I'm making," I say, though I can't quite form the words. My lips won't move properly and my throat is so dry. Leonid's face grows very large and the rest of the darkened room retreats behind him. Dr. Spizharny is now standing over me with a scalpel. The others have left, even Leonid, and just this doctor and another man, his assistant, are with me.

"Monsieur Scriabin," Dr. Spizharny says. "You must be still. We have to make an incision. It's the only way."

He lifts the sheet from my face and brings the scalpel close. I feel the blade slice into my lip and the wetness of blood flowing into my mouth as the other man quickly tries to staunch the bleeding. There is no new pain, just a slight release of pressure. The two men look at each other and frown.

"No pus," the assistant says.

Dr. Spizharny speaks to me again. "Monsieur Scriabin, we must make a deeper incision. Please, brace yourself. I'll do this quickly."

He slices again and I see blood spray upward. My face seems split in two and a jolt of pain surges through me, followed by a dull wave of throbbing in every nerve. I scream and the blood chokes me.

The room spins once more and the pain is gone. I'm formless again, basking in the grand kaleidoscope of Sasha's face.

"The time of Ecstasy is coming," he says, his voice echoing over a clash of wind and bells. "Surrender to me! Everything will be yours. Legions of feelings. Endless tides of divine power, of free will. You are eternal creation with no outward aim, no motive. A divine play with worlds past, worlds future. I give this all to you. I am your beloved freedom."

Then there is just a soft white light and silence. Soon, though, I hear Sasha whispering.

"I have created realities for you, my realities, but you can create your own. Whatever you desire, whatever you can imagine. You can live and relive, create endless worlds, endless realities. I give this to you."

"What's happened to my body?" I ask the light.

"The physical body is meaningless."

"It was raining. I was on a bench. Will I be all right?"

"You can live and die and live again. Think of some incident in that life that you wish to change. Go ahead."

I try to remember.

"Change it, reform it. Go ahead. Make yourself an Indian mystic. A child prodigy. A sacred prostitute in Ancient Rome. What stops you?"

"There's nothing. I see nothing. I remember nothing."

"You remember everything," he says, and before me, in the light, images form. In my mind, endless thoughts well up and shout at me for attention, for release. I focus on one of them—I'm sixteen years old and sitting on the piano bench in the living room. Karl sits next to me. It's late afternoon because the light from the windows is golden and washes everything. Karl is showing me how to play the simple part of a four-handed piano piece. He leans on my shoulder, inspecting my fingering. "Here," he says, placing his left hand over mine and putting his arm around my waist so he can reach my other hand. "Like this." I'm sixteen and I can barely breathe. Karl touches me—our hands, his arm and my waist, my body resting on his. I can't look anywhere but at our hands. Then he kisses my neck, softly. I close my eyes. His lips linger for a moment, then he stands up and quickly leaves the room. I don't move. We never speak of it again.

I can change things now. Replay the scene but keep his lips there longer. I could turn to him and kiss his mouth, then look into his eyes. I could.

"Yes," Sasha says. "Go on."

Karl's lips are on my neck. I see the yellow-tinged ivories of the keyboard, feel his arm. The moment stretches. His lips move up my neck, then he's gone. I've made him get up and leave, just as he'd done so many years ago.

"Why?" Sasha whispers. "Have you learned nothing?"

He's gone. The light is gone. Before me, once again, my memories play out, but I can't control them. My vision is split. I see myself, shivering on the bench in the rain, unable to move, a homeless lunatic that people pass by in disgust or pity and, simultaneously, I see another scene. There I am, there Michael is, on a train. He's exhausted, confused. He's just broken up with Paul. He's lost his job. He's heading back to his parents' house for his father's recital and because he has no place else to go. I watch this unfold before me as if I'm seeing it all for the first time.

3

Michael has not slept for two days. He is unshaven, unwashed, his clothes rumpled, his eyes a bit glazed and sunken, the skin under them dark. Occasionally, he mumbles to himself, then looks around the train car to see if anyone has noticed. He and Paul are finished, or at least that's how he understood their last argument. Not that it matters. Michael is on a train moving in the opposite direction, moving away from Paul, from his brainless job and those idiotic lawyers, leaving that tiny apartment and all his failures behind him. He's going to the recital. He's going to see his mother and father and Karl and Sara. And Amy. That was inevitable. Amy bored him. Sara hated him. Karl loved him, or used to.

I can make Karl love me again, though, he thought. I can show Sara and Dad and Mother, too.

The train rushes by fields of corn, the stalks yellow and broken, withering after the harvest. Michael knows the corn will be back next year. It will be reborn, just like he will. They all know he is coming, but he'd left town several days earlier than planned. What was there to stay for? They'll be surprised and delighted to see him so soon. Some of them, anyway. They'll act like they don't know anything about the real reason he's come, the real reason the recital is so monumental. Michael has suspected for a few days now, though he hasn't dared to say it out loud. They're going to ask him to play. It will be his concert hall debut. Dad will play a few pieces, then introduce him, call Michael onto the stage. He'll act surprised, of course, shocked but delighted. Michael tells the audience he'd been working on a piece by Scriabin. The Fifth Sonata. A murmur of excitement rolls through the crowd, followed by applause. Well, he tells them, if you really want to hear it.

Yes, they shout. Yes.

All right. But it's not quite perfect yet. Still. I suppose . . .

The applause grows.

Michael leans back in his seat as the train passes a small farming town. He will have to practice in secret at his parents' house. Mustn't spoil the surprise. Luckily, he'd learned how to practice in his head. Perhaps he should practice now, in front of the other passengers. He looks around.

Would you like to hear some Scriabin? He doesn't say it. He focuses and pushes the thought out to them.

No one looks at him or replies, but they don't have to. Michael can hear their thoughts coming back to him. Well, he imagines he does. He can't really read their minds. He laughs to himself. The man across the aisle stares at him for a moment, then looks away. Out the window, the cornfields turn into towns, which drop away to reveal more fields and occasionally windbreaks of trees.

Go ahead, look at me, Michael thinks. *What do you see? I can't read your mind. I'm not crazy.*

He makes a face when he's sure the man isn't looking. Michael closes his eyes, but he doesn't sleep. He sits completely still and begins to play Scriabin's Fifth Piano Sonata in his head.

Michael almost misses his stop, almost forgets his suitcase. He's been practicing and lost his sense of time. The section marked *vertiginoso con furio* was giving him problems. Was it *furio* enough?

He walks from the train station. It's growing dark and he notices the remains of snowbanks, pocked with soot, along the streets. He sighs. How come so much of the world has to be so ugly? Then he thinks of Paul. He had loved Paul. Paul had made the world seem beautiful sometimes. Michael stops, sets down his suitcase in the dirty snow, and cries.

Then it's over. Michael continues on his way, building happiness and excitement in his heart, manufacturing it so his parents won't suspect all the bungled chances he has left behind. He's starting over. This is Day One. He just needs some rest and time to practice. His suitcase grows heavier as he turns down a familiar street and approaches The House.

Marta answers the door. "Michael," she says, happy but confused.

"Hello, Mother. I forgot my key." He hugs her, which confuses her more.

"What's wrong?" she asks. "You look terrible. I thought you weren't coming home until Thursday."

Douglas has come into the entryway and looks at him cautiously.

"Dad!" Michael shouts and hugs him as well.

"Michael, darling, is everything all right?" Marta asks.

"This is a surprise," Douglas says.

"Mother, everything is fine." Michael's voice is too bright, too happy. "I took the week off. I wanted to spend more time with my family." He throws out his arms and tries to twirl around, but stumbles. The look on Marta's face is transparent: *He's drunk or on drugs.*

Douglas catches him.

"What's gotten into you?" he asks.

"Guess I'm just so excited . . . seeing my family . . . the recital. I haven't slept much."

"Well, let's get you to bed," Douglas says, starting to help him toward the stairs.

"I'm fine." Michael pulls away from Douglas. "But some sleep would be nice."

Marta just stares at him, which causes Michael to react. "What?" he asks rather sharply, then catches himself and smiles. "What's the matter, Mother?"

"You could use a shower," Marta says. "But I think you can take care of that tomorrow. I'll change the sheets in the morning."

"You do that," Michael says and begins to climb the stairs. Three steps up, he turns and asks, "Isn't anyone going to say, 'Welcome home'?"

Marta doesn't smile.

"Of course, darling. Welcome home," she says.

"Welcome home, son," Douglas says.

That's better, Michael thinks as he continues slowly upward.

Michael sleeps all day Sunday, finally emerging from his room at about four in the afternoon. He doesn't say much, answering Marta and Douglas's questions with groggy monosyllables, and returns to his room after dinner, where he sleeps until noon on Monday. His dreams are chaotic and vivid. In one, he plays the Fifth Sonata on a stage in the file room of Highsmith, Ripley, and Rendell. The audience includes Paul, Marta, Douglas, Sasha, the Franzes Liszt and Schubert, Colonel Pinkerton, Salomé, and Karl. The performance is repeatedly interrupted by the lawyers, who come in and crank the filing units. The audience doesn't seem to notice, but Michael has to stop and start again every time a file is retrieved. In another dream, his father plays the piano naked while Marta calmly bakes a pie.

When Michael wakes up on Monday, he doesn't leave his room except to visit the toilet. Marta waits for him in the hallway and asks if he's all right. He merely grumbles "Yeah" and goes back to his room while Marta tries to tell him that he needs to eat and shower. He ignores her, locking the bedroom door. The rest of the day, he practices the Fifth Sonata, lying naked on the bed, staring at the ceiling, his fingers twitching, his ears deaf to Marta and Douglas's knocking and frequent calls for him to come out. Occasionally he tells them he's fine just so they'll leave him alone. In the afternoon, he finds himself crying again, though he's not sure why. That evening, he accepts some dinner that Marta brings up on a tray and sets outside the door. All night he continues to practice, but drifts in and out of sleep until dawn.

On Tuesday morning he looks in the mirror and is horrified by the derelict he sees before him. His hair is greasy and matted, his eyes so sunken and the circles under them so dark that he thinks he may have died. He hasn't shaved since Friday and he notices his body is beginning to smell. He locks himself in the bathroom and showers, shaves, plucks, and moisturizes for two hours. When he emerges, his bed has been stripped and he can smell bacon frying downstairs.

Michael is euphoric and understands he must be on his best behavior but not give away that he knows the secret of the recital. He goes down to the kitchen and startles Marta with a hug. Michael knows she is happy that he's presentable again and tries to put her at ease by talking cheerfully about the recital and Scriabin's life. If Marta is disturbed by Michael's sudden change, she gives him no sign of it. She tells him his father is doing several interviews and won't be back until this afternoon.

"I thought we'd go for a drive," she says.

"Of course, Mother," Michael replies with a smile. "Whatever you want to do today." He's suspicious, but knows he mustn't show it.

Just a few minutes after they drive off, Michael understands that Marta is taking him to Dr. Jamison's office and feels superior, even a little sorry for her. He knows he's acted crazy, but he's an artist now and he has earned the right to some insanity. Douglas and Marta weren't prepared for it and now need to be sure Michael is well enough to play on Saturday. He'll indulge them this time, be on his best behavior, talk calmly with the good doctor.

They sit in the brown room and wait.

"It will be great to see Dr. Jamison again," Michael says to Marta. "It's been years."

"Just a chat," Marta says. "You seem a bit depressed."

"Depressed?" Michael chuckles and thinks of her as if she were an adorable, misinformed child. "I'm perfectly fine, but I'm happy to say hello to Dr. Jamison again. You do worry about me." He shakes his head and gives her a condescending little smile, though he suspects she isn't convinced. *She's just glad she got me here without hysterics,* he thinks.

"Do you still go to Dr. Jamison, Mother?" Michael asks. "How's *your* depression?"

On the bench, in the rain, Michael turns onto his stomach but doesn't wake up. I can see him, watch him twitch occasionally. No one has come along for a while. Gradually, imperceptibly, he grows smaller. I seem to be moving upward, farther away, higher into the sky. I continue watching him, even as the scene from his past plays, the images superimposing, though I can still separate them and switch between them at will.

"Michael," Dr. Jamison says, shaking his hand, "so good to see you again. It's been a while. How are you?"

"Fine," Michael replies. "I'm great. And you're looking quite handsome, Doctor. Have you been working out?" He hopes to fluster Dr. Jamison, slather on compliments and confuse him, but Dr. Jamison, as Michael soon remembers, is unflappable.

"Thank you, Michael. I still swim laps. Have a seat."

They both sit down and smile at each other before Dr. Jamison makes the first move.

"Your mother tells me you seemed depressed the past few days. Anything you'd like to talk about?"

Michael remembers how much he wanted Dr. Jamison when he was seeing him regularly. He was depressed then, right out of college with no job, no boyfriend, no prospects for either. He remembers how he wished he could touch the soft gray hair, feel that beautiful beard against his cheek. Everyone falls in love with the psychiatrist, but that banal fact didn't keep Michael from fantasizing and scheming about how they would first touch. He doesn't have those pangs of love and need anymore, though he still wouldn't mind seeing Dr. Jamison naked.

"I've never been better," Michael says. "You know how my mother is. Always worrying."

Dr. Jamison nods. "Everything going well at home? Where do you live now?"

"Near the university with my partner Paul. We're very happy. I work at a law firm, in the records department, but I'm going to quit soon."

"Oh?" Dr. Jamison's eyebrows arch. "And do what?"

Michael laughs. "I'm a musician."

"Really? Your mother didn't tell me. What sort of musician?"

"Why don't you ask my mother? You two seem to talk about me quite a bit." Michael's smile doesn't falter, though Dr. Jamison is beginning to annoy him. All at once, however, Michael understands. Dr. Jamison wants to have sex with him, right in his office. All of this was just a pretext to get him here. It was Dr. Jamison who called when he heard Michael was going to play at the recital.

"We don't talk about you that much, Michael. Your mother is just concerned. What instrument do you play?"

Michael's smile grows languid. He slouches in his chair and stretches out his legs.

"Listen, Frank," he says. "I can call you Frank, can't I?"

"Of course."

"I appreciate all the trouble you've gone through. Really, it's very flattering. But, Frank, it's just not the right time or place."

"I'm afraid I don't understand."

"Well," Michael lowers his voice to a stage whisper, "I couldn't possibly have sex with you now. Not with Mother right outside."

Dr. Jamison's smile doesn't move, but his eyes tell Michael that he's made a mistake. This isn't about sex at all.

"Now, Michael, you know we can't have sex. You're a patient of mine. Is that why you think you're here? Sex?"

"I'm not your patient," Michael says and his voice is hard and angry. "There's nothing wrong with me. I'm not anyone's patient." He stands.

"Michael, let's talk about that for a minute."

"I'm not going to talk to you anymore," Michael says as he opens the door. "Why don't you talk to my mother instead?"

He walks down the hall and pauses at the waiting-room door.

"The doctor's ready for you, Mother," Michael says to Marta, who looks up from her magazine, startled to see him so soon. "You two can talk about me all you want now. Oh, and Mother, I came home for the recital. I can just as easily leave before it takes place if you don't like my behavior. I'm not the one that needs to talk to a shrink." He leaves the doctor's building and starts walking and mumbling to himself. He'd lost it in there, but how could they do this to him when he was getting ready to play? Artists are difficult, so what? And who the hell does Jamison think he is? If they would just leave him alone, he could concentrate.

"I can't fucking concentrate!" Michael shouts at a passing car.

I really should leave, he thinks. Wouldn't that screw up everything. No recital, no surprise. But where would he go? Not back to Paul. Not after the things that were said. To Karl? Michael isn't quite sure that would work out. Karl would tell Amy, who would report every-thing back to Mother. *I need more practice,* Michael thinks. *That's when I'm calm, when I'm sitting or lying with my eyes closed and playing the piano in my head.* He just thinks about the music then, not about his parents or work or Paul. But the job is gone now. So is Paul. There's no use thinking about him. Unless. Unless the fight was part of this elabo-rate surprise. Unless Paul had staged the whole thing and would be in the audience on Saturday. Artists need torment and sadness. Paul knows this and was trying to help. On Saturday, Michael will play with a passion and a dark fury because he'll think he's lost Paul's love, but afterward, after the people mill around backstage to congratulate him, the crowd will part and reveal Paul standing there. Michael will run to him and they'll embrace.

If this is the case, then Michael can't let on. He has to stay sad and tormented or the music will suffer. Now everything seems to fall into place and Michael realizes he should have played along with Dr. Jamison. He should have been depressed and sad so everyone would know he will play beautifully. Michael congratulates himself for stay-ing one step ahead of them all. He stops, then turns around and walks back to Dr. Jamison and his mother, telling himself to stop smiling now. He must be tormented. He must do it or the music will suffer.

Dr. Jamison prescribes some pills after Michael tells him about the breakup and the loss of his job. Michael knows he's not really supposed to take the pills—that could hurt his playing—but he sees the pre-scription as proof he's convinced them all. He didn't have any prob-lem acting depressed, especially once he started talking about Paul. He even cried, though that surprised him a bit. The tears came so eas-ily.

At home, Marta gives him the pills, which he keeps under his tongue, then spits out in his hand when she's not looking. *Of course, she knows I'm doing this,* he thinks and tries not to laugh. He stays in his room the rest of the day and all day Wednesday and Thursday, feign-ing drowsiness from the pills, which Marta gives him religiously twice a day. He spends a lot of time drifting in and out of sleep when he's not practicing, though Michael finds he's having trouble distinguishing between the two states. Several times, he accidentally swallows the pills and has to force himself to vomit quietly so Marta and Douglas will not hear. Douglas comes up and visits Michael. He seems uncomfortable and doesn't stay long and Michael wonders if it's because Douglas worries the pills will affect Michael's ability to play. *Surely they've told him,* Michael thinks. *Surely he knows.*

"Everything will be fine," Michael tells him. "Don't worry."

"Of course it will be," Douglas says. "I'm just so glad you'll be there. It means a lot to me."

Michael is euphoric, in awe of the love everyone has for him and the elaborate schemes they have planned to prove it.

"It means a lot to me, too." He doesn't feel badly that he has so little love to return. It's as if every emotion and passion he has is focused inward and directed at the music. There seems to be nothing left for people—not even for Paul right now.

When Michael wakes up Friday morning, something seems wrong. The sunlight has a dull green tinge to it that makes his head pound. He tries to practice, but the light interferes. Even with the shades drawn, some of the light leaks in and ruins everything. He realizes that Sasha has not come to him since he's been home, except once as part of a dream, but there have been no visitations. Was it a sign that Michael has learned everything there was to learn or did it mean Sasha had abandoned him? Was the Time of Ecstasy at hand or had Michael lost the way? He tries to practice again, but the music won't come, so he panics, paces his room, his fingers twitching wildly, his head nodding as if he were praying. *I have done something wrong,* he thinks.

He hears voices downstairs, so soft he stops pacing and just listens to be sure they are real. Carefully, he opens his door and walks to the head of the stairs as though he was stepping amid soap bubbles and must not break them. The voices are real. Douglas and Marta are talking downstairs. They're talking about Michael.

"It's your big night," Douglas says. "We'll all keep our eyes on him."

"Maybe he shouldn't be out in public."

"He's on medication. He's doing well. Karl and I can watch him."

"Oh, God." Marta sighs.

"You shouldn't have to do it all by yourself. We're here."

"What a mess he's made of himself," Marta says, her voice so tired.

It all sounds so convincing. Michael had forgotten about Marta's opening and is now a little angry with her. *She's the mess,* he thinks. *She's the one who needs more extensive treatment.* He wants to scream. He can feel it sitting inside him, waiting. *I should spoil your stupid opening. It would serve you right.* He creeps back to his room and tries to practice, but nothing comes. Perhaps he's trying too hard, so he decides to shower, shave, go about the day as normally as he can, spitting out the pills, pretending to be interested in the lives around him—in Marta's opening and Douglas's recital—pretending he knows nothing about the surprise tomorrow night. His night. He breathes deeply and tells himself Sasha has not deserted him. He just needs to relax. He needs to breathe.

Michael and the bench grow smaller still. He's shivering now. No one stops to help him. The sun is setting. The rain has finally ended. If I focus, I can stop my movement upward, keep him from moving too far away. From this height, I can see the house where their apartment is. I can see the university, the whole town. Paul is out there somewhere. The upward pull is strong, though. The other memories tear at me and soon Michael is moving away again.

The opening is crowded with well-dressed people and other more eccentric types. There is a crowd around Marta, who never stops talking. She's wearing a long black dress with a high collar and no sleeves, a simple strand of pearls around her neck. On the walls are her starscapes—nebulae, galaxies, constellations, planets—carefully lit and arranged. Douglas moves from group to group, a celebrity here as well. Sara pontificates to three young men, conspicuously ignoring Michael, who stands by a large painting called *Starbirth,* which shows the Horsehead nebula twinkling with newly formed stars. Karl and Amy try to engage him in a conversation about paralegal work, while Michael clutches a wine glass filled with cola.

"You don't have to baby-sit me, Karl," Michael says.

"Who's baby-sitting?" Karl asks, feigning hurt.

"We haven't seen you for months," Amy says.

"I'd like to walk around some, look at the paintings," Michael tells them. "That's OK, isn't it?" His sarcasm makes Amy blush.

"Sure, Mikey." Karl seems offended now. "Come on, honey. Let's go freshen our drinks and say hi to Sara." He takes Amy's arm and moves away.

Michael just keeps standing where he is but thinks how ridiculous Marta's paintings are. Like comic book versions of the real thing.

"You look as bored as I am," someone says to him.

A man is standing next to Michael, admiring him as if he were a painting. The man is about forty, shorter than Michael, with a shaved head and a little beard on his chin. He wears an expensive black sports coat, black jeans, and a black T-shirt that fits tightly over his muscular chest. His lopsided smile is disarming, as are his eyes, which look blue one moment, green the next. Michael is drawn to the man's eyes. They remind him of Sasha.

"Well," Michael says, "it's just that I thought there would be art here."

The man snickers and looks at the painting behind Michael, stepping back a bit and studying it with an exaggerated stance, stroking his chin.

"*Starbirth*," he says. "Hmmmm. Looks like it belongs in a comic book, not a gallery."

Now Michael laughs. "That's exactly what I was thinking."

"Great minds think alike," the man says with a smile, then extends his hand to Michael. "Justin LeBruin," he says.

Michael hesitates, then clasps the man's hand. "Paul," he says. Justin's hand is strong and warm. "Paul . . . Alexander." Justin holds Michael's hand just a little longer than normal, then slowly releases it, all the while examining Michael's face.

"Are you an artist?" Michael asks.

"Yes," Justin says. "I paint. And you?"

"A musician. A pianist, actually." Michael is giddy.

"Really? Let me see your hands." Justin takes his hand and spreads out his fingers, gently stroking Michael's palm. A shiver runs up Michael's back. "Yes," Justin says. "Long, beautiful fingers. I play as well, but only for relaxation. My fingers are too stubby."

As they stand there, touching palm to palm, Michael decides he will have sex with Justin. It's a simple decision. He glances at Marta and Douglas, who are surrounded by groups of people and oblivious to him. Karl and Amy have disappeared, swallowed up by the crowd. Sara's caustic laugh can be heard rising above the din of conversations.

"Listen, Paul," Justin says. "This place is dreary. My studio is just a few blocks away. We could have some good wine, talk about art and music."

"I'd love to," Michael says and they are gone without anyone noticing.

"Go ahead and play if you want," Justin says, gesturing toward the grand piano in the center of his enormous loft. He is pouring two glasses of wine in the kitchen area as Michael gazes out a window that takes up an entire wall. The city's lights are spread out before him. He can see a cleaning crew moving through an empty office space in a nearby skyscraper. The cars below him on the streets flow in lighted patterns.

"This is an amazing view," Michael says, very softly.

Justin is behind him, brushing against his back, then offers Michael his wine.

"The daylight is perfect for work," Justin says. "At night, I love watching the city come alive and then go to sleep."

They clink their glasses in a toast.

"To music," Justin says. "And to handsome musicians."

Michael blushes. "To art," he says.

"You seem a little nervous."

Michael takes a sip of wine and shakes his head. "No," he says. "Just a little shy is all."

"I find that so sexy," Justin says, as Michael knew he would. Michael plays a role: little boy lost in the big city. Justin responds in kind: mentor/teacher/protector/violator.

I don't want to watch the rest of this, but I have no choice. It's so sad and predictable. I shift my concentration to Michael on the bench and let the memory of Justin and the other Michael occupy the periphery of my consciousness. I stop my upward movement again, put all my energy into staying still, floating above the town like a kite. In Justin's loft, there is cocaine and flesh and sex. Tongues, nipples, muscles, penises, asses. It divides my attention. I try to move down, back toward the bench and the park, but the other memory prevents me. The sex goes on too long, the cocaine preventing either man from reaching orgasm. Finally, while Justin is pumping away, Michael looks at his face. Their eyes meet and, for an instant, Justin changes into Sasha. Michael shouts and begins an orgasm that seems to last minutes. His vision blurs. His body goes numb.

I start to move upward again. I try to keep Michael from slipping away, but the other Michael's cocaine-addled brain is flashing and racing and throwing me off. He's babbling, shrieking, crying, laughing, but not saying a word as his heartbeat gradually slows. Then he's lying next to Justin, the lights from the skyscrapers and the shadows cast by candles flickering across their bodies.

He hears music in his head again. Justin runs his hand slowly across Michael's chest and moves closer.

"I have to go," Michael says. Justin's touch is suddenly unbearable to him.

"What for?" Justin whispers and licks Michael's neck, which sends a clanging dissonance through him and stops the music. He gets out of bed and begins looking for his clothes scattered around the room.

"I have friends at the gallery," he says. "They'll be wondering what happened to me."

He looks at the clock and knows the reception has ended. Marta and Douglas must be frantic, he thinks with a mixture of glee and dread. It serves them right.

"Call them in the morning," Justin says. "You're a big boy. Tell them you were kidnapped and ravished."

Michael can't concentrate and keeps picking up and setting down pieces of clothes without getting dressed.

"I wasn't tied up," he says, finally pulling on his pants.

"Come back to bed and I'll see what I can do."

"Another time." Michael leans down to kiss Justin good-bye and Justin grabs him, tries to pull him back into bed.

"No," Michael says and struggles. Justin laughs and pulls harder. "Stop it!" Michael screams and starts flailing his arms, hitting Justin.

"What the fuck is wrong with you?" Justin's mood has changed as quickly as Michael's. He jumps out of bed and slaps Michael hard across the face. They stand there looking at each other, chests heaving, and a wave of remorse and guilt overtakes Michael. *I've done something wrong,* he thinks. *I've screwed everything up. I've been so stupid. I love Paul, but how can he love me after everything I've done?* Without another word, Michael finishes dressing, takes his coat, and leaves. Justin just stands there glowering at him, naked and glistening in the candlelight.

"Oh, thank God," Douglas says when Michael walks through the gallery doors. The place is deserted except for Marta and Douglas and Karl and Amy.

"Are you all right?" Karl asks, coming over to Michael and putting his arm around him, as if he might fall down without support.

"I went for a walk," Michael says. "I got confused." He leans into Karl, loving his solidity, feeling pitiful.

Marta gives Karl a look that says, *He was your responsibility. You have disappointed me.* Karl squeezes Michael a little harder.

"Come on, Mikey," he says. "You look tired."

"I'll get the car," Douglas says.

Michael hugs Karl. His head, which moments before had been clear from the cold night air, is now growing fuzzy.

"Honey," Karl says to Amy. "Can you go with Dad and get ours?" *Send her away,* Michael thinks. *Stay here and help me through all this.* Karl digs in his pocket and hands the keys to Amy. He gives her a quick kiss and Michael, his head on Karl's shoulder, his eyes closed, feels the kiss all through his body, warming him like a sip of brandy. He pictures himself and Karl in the backseat of Douglas's car, being driven home through the wind-swept, deserted streets, Michael's face pressed to Karl's chest as Karl holds him. He'd listen to Karl's steady breathing say *Rest now,* say *You're forgiven,* say *Don't go.* The cold air hits Michael as Karl helps him outside and slides him into the backseat, leaving him to lie alone while Karl goes to another car, where Amy waits, and drives off. It's Amy who will lie with her face on Karl's chest, who'll smell the scent of his skin and hear the messages in his breath as he sleeps. Michael tries to be happy for her. He watches the streetlights and the tops of buildings slip by as he begins to erase the evening from his memory. His mind still moves so quickly, though, and he's convinced he won't sleep for days.

Michael finally drifts into a light and fitful slumber near dawn that leaves him exhausted when he wakes at noon. Marta and Douglas check in on him, bring him meals and pills, but leave him to rest in the darkened bedroom. A clinging, metallic taste at the back of his mouth and in his throat from the cocaine persists through much of the day. He drinks glass after glass of water. Despite feeling so bad, however, Michael is relieved to find that the music has returned again and that he can practice fairly well. He is nervous about the recital for the first time and is uneasy that he's been away from a piano for over a week, wanting the proximity of the instrument so he can absorb its energy and feel the secret vibrations of its silent strings. Yet the physicality of the piano has little to do with the music, which exists outside of time and space. Sasha showed him, revealed the secrets to him, and Michael saw that he could channel the music directly from his mind into the instrument. Tonight, at the recital, he would show everyone else. They would hear Scriabin's Fifth Sonata as it had never been heard before.

"Why did you trick me that night?" I push the thought into the void. I can sense the emptiness out beyond the images of my memory. Sasha is waiting there, silent, merciless. "Why did you set me up?"

With each thought, I move farther away from Michael, who is indistinguishable from the trees and grasses of the park now. The other Michael is getting out of bed, responding to Marta's urgings. Douglas will meet them at the restaurant for a light dinner before the recital. Michael moves slowly, allowing the stream of water in the shower to wash away the film of regret and pain that the past few days have deposited on him. In the hiss of the spray, the music stays with him. It's there in the dripping of the showerhead, in the sounds of his bare feet on the tile floor, in the rasp of the towel on his skin.

He looks in the mirror. At first he simply assesses his appearance— a little haggard, the skin under his eyes a bit baggy, his face blotchy. It's disappointing but he knows that once he steps on stage, none of that will matter. He pushes his hair around, examines his teeth, then, as if he were a windup toy whose spring had finally unwound, Michael's movements cease and he stares into his own eyes. They are not the disarming blue of Karl's eyes, the shifting agate of Sasha's, the deep, somber hazel of Douglas's, or the pale blue of Paul's. They're brown. *Like the color of a sofa you barely notice,* he thinks. *Like a clump of dry dirt.* In the pit of his stomach, Michael feels the beginning of a flutter, then tenses as a wave of panic overcomes him. Nothing shows in his eyes. For a moment he is completely lucid—horribly, blatantly clearheaded—and he remembers leaving Paul and how he ended up here, in the bathroom of his parents' house, looking in a mirror he's looked into day after day for more than half of his remembered life. He wants to scream, not from anger or fear, but from spite and envy and a string of bad choices that each seemed so right and good once.

Finally, the spell is broken, and Michael hears the music again. Everything has been leading up to tonight, he knows. He feels it all through his body like a warm, steady glow.

In his room he looks through the few clothes he's brought with him, none of which seems appropriate for being on stage, but he knows he needs to look as though he hadn't suspected they'd ask him to play. He'd wear a white oxford shirt, dark blue slacks, and, in a gesture that seems appropriate, he'd borrow one of Douglas's ties.

At the restaurant, Michael asks if he can go backstage before the recital and see the piano. He wants to touch it, to see it glow.

In the car on the way to the theater, Michael practices the piece again and again in his mind. His fingers twitch in time to the music.

Backstage, Michael hears the audience. The gleaming piano sits behind the curtains like a statue about to be unveiled. As he approaches it, the strings vibrate. At his touch, the ivory of the keys grows brighter. He doesn't bring his finger down, for to sound a note now would be sacrilege.

In his seat, Michael surveys the theater. It is sumptuous but not large, decorated with elaborate cornices and pilasters in a faux-Egyptian style. The curtain is deep red velvet. There are six steps up to the stage. Michael is seated at the end of a row, not because he asked to be but because Marta suggested it. Sara has brought a date, a fleshy, fresh-faced blond who looks like a German soldier, and sits farthest from Michael. Next is Amy, then Karl, who seems less at ease than usual. Marta sits at Michael's side. He's not sure when they will call him to the stage.

The lights dim. The crowd murmurs. As the curtain rises, Douglas enters from the left to loud applause. He bows, so crisp and distinguished in his tuxedo. On his face is a small, appreciative smile.

Douglas plays one piece, then a second. Michael doesn't listen to them. He feels a surge of nervousness, then a floating calm as the audience applauds. Douglas pauses before the third piece, hands in his lap as though saying a brief prayer, then, with a quick, decisive movement of his hands and upper body, he begins to play.

There is a familiar growling in the low keys, then Douglas's hands fly up the keyboard and after a brief pause, begin a soft musing. The theater falls away in front of Michael, his peripheral vision goes black. For a moment, Michael doesn't understand what is happening, then the sound, the light, the world comes rushing in with a furious, horrible weight.

He screams.

4

The images are gone. I hang in a black void, sending thoughts out all around me like a forgotten beacon drifting at the edge of a galaxy. Sasha doesn't answer. Perhaps I've been calling out to him for minutes, perhaps centuries. I exist, not sure where I end and the void begins. Perhaps I have become the void. Perhaps there is no Michael, no Sasha. Perhaps there never was.

I'm cold. I have no body, no nerves, no blood, no skin to distinguish temperature. Still this illusion of cold persists.

I begin to think about light and gradually, all around me, faint dots appear out of the void, growing in intensity until they are stars. The Void becomes Space. I choose one of the stars, a bright one to my left, and will it closer. It grows large and planets move by me until I recognize Saturn and Jupiter. I'm warmer now as I pass Mars and approach the blue-and-white orb of Earth. Without fear, I move closer to it until it fills my vision and at a certain point I begin to distinguish up and down. I see the familiar shape of North America, focus in and move down and down through the thickening atmosphere and clouds until I can make out landforms and roads and cities. There is the town I once lived in; there is the park. Michael still lies on the bench.

The rain has slowed to a drizzle and the sun is gone, but a bright half-moon shines through the gaps in the clouds.

I move in closer. Someone has thrown an old blanket over Michael. Surely Paul has gone looking for him or called the police. Surely something will be done.

As I float above the town, I can see the evidence of other lives, cars pulling into driveways, students with backpacks and umbrellas walking to and from campus, lights going on in houses, the blue glow of televisions, the buzz of conversations and arguments and monologues, the barking of dogs, the whisper of tree branches in the wind, an occasional shout, music playing. An evening in spring, when the day is still too short and the weather untrustworthy, can be, I remember, so dreary. One feels stuck in a routine, robbed of daylight, convinced things will never change, though change is everywhere—in the smell of the air, in the dormant trees coming to life, everywhere. From up here, though, the evening is a deep, magical blue and the lights from buildings and streets and cars glow and twinkle. Am I, in my formlessness and omniscience, so naive, so nostalgic? From on high, everything has a place and a pattern. It's only when you're close that the ugliness, the banality is clear, that the patterns become repetitive and deadening, unwavering, unbreakable. Up here, everything seems possible. But down there . . .

Down there, Michael lies on a bench. Maybe he's dying or ill. Maybe he's hopeless or insane. Maybe he'll recover, remember his life, and everything will be as it was. His life will go on.

Then my vision is split again. I see Michael, much older. He lives alone in a small apartment with three cats and piles of newspapers carefully sorted and stacked by some system known only to him. His face is deeply wrinkled, his teeth yellowed, his hairline has receded halfway up his head. He talks to himself and his cats and to others who aren't there. He's obese, hasn't shaved or washed in weeks. Under his unmade bed is a pile of pornographic magazines.

Someone is giggling. All around me, inside me, over me, under me is the sound of Sasha laughing.

I focus on the park and with an effort I replace the image of future-Michael with another image of the park. Now I float above two parks, two towns, two worlds. Keeping one world as is, I push. I focus down on the other, magnifying the park. I'm in a tree. I'm on the ground. I grow smaller and smaller until the brown winter grass looms over me and I can hear the rumble of earthworms as they tunnel and swallow and defecate. I look up between the gigantic fronds of grass and see the moon.

Split, I am in both places. I see both skies. They are nothing alike, yet they are the same sky, the same clouds, the same moon.

Create, Sasha had said, revise, distort, obliterate.

I split my focus. I push in both worlds. I push upward and downward. Slowly, each of me begins to move toward the other. Obliterate. Cancel. Revise. Create. With each inch, it becomes easier and my speed increases until I careen toward myself and we meet somewhere over Michael and the bench with a flash, then fall together like a fine rain.

5

I'm drifting awake. It doesn't happen all at once. I feel the thin bedsheets against my legs and arms. On the other side of a wall, people are talking. I can't hear the words. Someone moves near me and I open my eyes.

I'm in a hospital room again. A middle-aged woman with shiny black hair smiles at me. She's wearing a nurse's uniform.

"How are you feeling?" she asks.

I nod. A tube runs into my arm.

"Just some fluids," she says and checks my bedpan. "You were a bit dehydrated. Do you need anything?"

I shake my head and she's gone.

I don't remember coming to the hospital. I was in the apartment, lying in bed. Paul had just left for work or class. Had we quarreled? I remember being upset. How did I end up in a hospital again?

Paul comes into the room. He stays near the door.

"Hey," he says, smiling a little. He looks as though he hasn't slept for a while. "The police found you unconscious in the park."

I can't look at him. "I don't remember." I'm so sick of saying that, so sick of excuses.

"Yeah," Paul says. "I figured as much. I called the police when I got home and you were gone."

We don't speak for a while, then Paul says, "Look, you're tired. I'll leave you alone."

"No," I say and turn to look at him. "Can't you stay?"

There's no smile now, just an exhausted sadness in his eyes.

"Sure," he says, coming over to the bed. He leans down and kisses my forehead. "Just for a bit." He holds my hand.

"When can I go home?"

Paul is silent for a moment. "It's complicated. I called your parents. We all agree you need some help—more than I can give you. I can't stay with you all day, Mike. You need someone around."

"So . . ."

"We all think you're better off here for a while. Dr. Hammond will be treating you."

I squeeze Paul's hand. My eyes burn, and I can't stop a tear from welling up and falling on my hospital gown.

"Come on, Mike. It's just for a while. Then you can go home."

Which home, I wonder. Paul should have said, *You can come home with me.* I suspect he's given up. Right now, I can't blame him. All I can do is get better and help him change his mind.

"Will you visit me?" I ask.

"Of course."

You'll visit me every day, I think, but I can't say the words. I know. Things will be different now. I just know.

"Your mother's here," Paul says. "Staying at a hotel. I called her." He makes a move to pull away, but I won't let go of his hand. "Your dad is touring."

"Hold me," I say. "Can you? Please?"

In Paul's eyes, I see thoughts flash. He loves me. He hates me. I disgust him. I amuse him. I fill him with dread. He sits down and his arms enfold me. I lean in toward his heart, rest my head on his chest. I listen, hearing reluctance or maybe caution in his heartbeat, like a buzz in his blood. Someday, I want to take care of Paul just as he's taking care of me. I never had the chance to care for him. I couldn't lift my head and look around to see when he needed me. I want to tell him this, but how can I? I don't think he likes me much right now.

Paul gets up, but stays by my bed, looking at me. "Mike, I want you to get better. We all do. Your parents and I want the same thing for you now."

"Do you want me back?"

Now he looks at a corner of the room, at a chair, at anything but me. "You'll have to stay here for a while," he says. "Let's talk about that later, Mike. OK?"

I hear the room buzz, sounding just like Paul's blood, and I wonder what I can do to help him. He's so tired and pale. He's just as hurt, just as damaged as I am. But you have to look close to see it. He functions. He hides his damage and goes on.

"Your mother should be here any minute," he says.

"How do I look?"

"Like you've been sleeping outside in the rain before you were brought in to the hospital. You look like shit."

I smile. Perhaps I can help him. Perhaps I can give him up so he can come back to me. I'm someone he pities now. How can you love someone you feel that way about? You can't.

"When I'm out of here," I say and Paul listens. He leans in, but this time I look away. "I could stay with Mother and Dad for a while. Until I'm on my feet."

"We can talk about it later," he says. He kisses my forehead.

I don't say anything, but I want to tell him. Soon, I'll be better. One day, when we least expect it, everything will come back to me. Some chemical will trigger another chemical in my brain and start a reaction that will change the way I think, the way I see the world. I'll stop noticing myself so much. I'll respond to other people, wanting to know what they're feeling, intrigued by their plights and dreams.

Mother walks into the room. She comes to the bedside and touches my arm. Her glasses are large and slightly blue. For a moment she just looks at me.

"Michael," she says. The sound of my name comes out of her like a sigh.

"Mother, I'm sorry," I say. "It won't happen again."

Her lips tighten, and I can tell she's trying not to cry, trying to believe me.

"I'll come home with you," I tell her. My mouth is dry and my voice cracks. I'm speaking the truth, speaking it so plainly that I ache and a strange thing happens: I can imagine the future.

I see myself. One day, months from now, I walk down a busy street, crowded with people on their way somewhere. I see an old woman standing on the corner, confused, unsure where she should go or what she should do. I recognize the look on her face. I know what she's feeling.

"Let me help you," I say.

She whispers, "I can't remember anything. I can't remember my name or where I'm going."

I stay with her. Talk to her. We go to a coffee shop and sit until she remembers where she is going and what she's called.

"I know all about it," I tell her. "I know what it's like. And it will pass."

One day, months from now, in our apartment, I sit next to Paul on the piano bench. The light from the windows turns everything yellow, yet nothing glows. The piano makes no sound unless we touch the keys. There's just the golden light and the warmth of Paul sitting next to me, leaning his body into mine. My fingers are poised, and I wait. Paul kisses my neck, his lips lingering there. One by one, I bring my fingers down until I play some shimmering chord.

acknowledgments

Without the friendship, critical acumen, and emotional support of Brian Bouldrey and Jean Thompson, I doubt this book would ever have been finished.

I'd also like to thank Stephen Beachy, Doug Coupland, Robert Drake, and Terry Wolverton for offering suggestions or encouragement at various stages of the novel's development.

It is a writer's dream to be given time and space to work. I am particularly indebted to Dorland Mountain Arts Colony in Temecula, California, for granting me a residency during which I finished a draft of this novel. I'm convinced that any beauty to be found in its pages is the result of the time I spent among the oak trees, agaves, and coyotes at Dorland. Special thanks to Karen Parrot and Robert Willis for helping make my time at Dorland so rewarding.

I was also fortunate to be granted a residency at the Atlantic Center for the Arts in New Smyrna Beach, Florida, which allowed me time to revise the book and mingle with some very talented writers, graphic artists, and musicians.

a note on sources

The genesis of this novel was an interview I read in Jonathan Ned Katz's groundbreaking *Gay American History*. Katz interviewed an anonymous gay man who had been institutionalized in the early 1960s. I used some of this man's symptoms and pain in forming the character of Michael Van Allen but quickly left any resemblance to the real-life situation behind as Michael took on a life of his own and moved into the twenty-first century.

Alexander Scriabin was a real person, considered by many to be one of the greatest pianists and most influential composers of the early twentieth century. Although I have used him in a fictional context, I attempted to stay as close to the facts as possible. I relied on several books and articles for the details of Scriabin's life, primarily *Scriabin: A Biography* by Faubion Bowers, a rewarding and vastly entertaining work which contains the translations of some of Scriabin's notebooks and poetry that I have quoted and paraphrased in this novel. Other works that helped me understand Scriabin's philosophy, music, and times include *Scriabin: Artist and Mystic* by Boris de Schloezer (translated by Nicolas Slonimsky), *Scriabin* by Alfred J. Swan, *Daily Life in Russia Under the Last Tsar* by Henri Troylat (translated by Malcolm Barnes), Faubion Bowers's preface to the Dover Press score of Scriabin's *Poem of Ecstasy* and his translation of Scriabin's poem in the same volume, Hugh Macdonald's liner notes for Giuseppe Sinopoli's 1988 recording of *Poem of Ecstasy* with the New York Philharmonic, and Nicolas Slonimsky's insightful article in the San Francisco Symphony's program for the January 1995 performance of *Poem of Ecstasy*.

ABOUT THE AUTHOR

Jim Tushinski's fiction has appeared in the anthologies *His 3* and *Quickies* as well as in literary journals, including *The Blithe House Quarterly*, *Harrington Gay Men's Fiction Quarterly*, and *The James White Review*. Jim has also written book reviews and feature articles for *The San Francisco Bay Guardian*, *Lambda Literary Report*, *Bay Area Reporter*, and the *San Francisco Sentinel*.

Jim's short video "Jan-Michael Vincent Is My Muse," which he wrote, produced, and directed, has screened internationally and has been the official selection at over twenty-five film festivals. Jim is currently working on a new novel and a new film project.